"I honestly don't understand what's going on," I said. "I love this neighborhood. I love being close to businesses and people and still having privacy." I paused. "I know it isn't as fancy as the subdivision where I was renting, but…it makes me happy."

"That's what's important." Stephanie stood up and gave me a hug. "Besides, at least you haven't found any dead bodies in this neighborhood." She smiled before adding. "Yet."

I was silent for several moments.

"I was just kidding, Mom."

"I'm sorry, dear. I was just thinking. You know, I don't believe in coincidences, but I haven't had any problems until Archibald Lowry was murdered two days ago. Since then, someone has tried to steal Rex and an intruder has gotten into my backyard." I shook my head. "I may not have discovered a dead body, but I think I'm going to need to find a killer if I want to have peace."

"Alright, Sherlock." Stephanie clapped her hands. "Let's get this investigation underway!"

Books by V.M. Burns

Mystery Bookshop Series
THE PLOT IS MURDER
READ HERRING HUNT
THE NOVEL ART OF MURDER
WED, READ & DEAD
BOOKMARKED FOR MURDER

Dog Club Series
IN THE DOG HOUSE
THE PUPPY WHO KNEW TOO MUCH
BARK IF IT'S MURDER
PAW AND ORDER

Published by Kensington Publishing Corporation

Paw and Order

V.M. Burns

LYRICAL UNDERGROUND
Kensington Publishing Corp.
www.kensingtonbooks.com

LYRICAL UNDERGROUND BOOKS are published by

Kensington Publishing Corp.
119 West 40th Street
New York, NY 10018

All Kensington titles, imprints, and distributed lines are available at special quantity discounts for bulk purchases for sales promotion, premiums, fund-raising, educational, or institutional use.

Special book excerpts or customized printings can also be created to fit specific needs. For details, write or phone the office of the Kensington Sales Manager: Kensington Publishing Corp., 119 West 40th Street, New York, NY 10018. Attn. Sales Department. Phone: 1-800-221-2647.

Lyrical Underground and Lyrical Underground logo Reg. US Pat. & TM Off.

First Electronic Edition: August 2020
ISBN-13: 978-1-5161-0993-7 (ebook)
ISBN-10: 1-5161-0993-7 (ebook)

First Print Edition: August 2020
ISBN-13: 978-1-5161-0994-4
ISBN-10: 1-5161-0994-5

Printed in the United States of America

Acknowledgments

Thank you to John Scognamiglio and everyone from Kensington, and to Dawn Dowdle at Blue Ridge Literary Agency.

Thanks to my fantastic work family: Linda Kay, Monica Jill, Tim, Chuck, Lindsey, Kristie and Sandy. Thank you to my wonderful team: Amber, Derrick, Eric, Jennifer, and Robin. Plus, special thanks to the wonderful training team who have done so much to support and promote my books: Grace, Deborah, Tena, and Jamie. Thanks to Abby Vandiver, Alexia Gordon, and E.L. Reddick for legal and medical advice. Thank you Lori Boness Caswell for coming up with the name.

As always, special thanks to my family and to my good friends, Shelitha Mckee and Sophia Muckerson.

Special thanks to Addison Abbott for allowing me to include you as a character in this book.

Chapter 1

"We need to talk," I whispered into the ear of my best friend, Dixie.

Scarlett Jefferson, Dixie to her friends, was just about to take a sip of champagne from a beautiful fluted glass. However, after one glance at my face, she handed her glass to her husband, Beau, who was standing nearby.

I gave my date, Dennis Olson, although everyone called him Red, a look that I hope said, *I'm really sorry.*

It must have worked because he mouthed the words, "You owe me." Then he tugged again at the collar of his tuxedo.

I grabbed Dixie by the arm and pulled her away.

The Chattanooga Museum was packed with guests for the Eastern Tennessee Poodle Rescue Association's fundraiser, but as a museum employee I knew about several secret alcoves in areas the general public were unlikely to stumble across, and I headed for the nearest one. When we got to a dimly lit area that featured glass sculptures, I stopped.

Dixie stared. "Now, what's so important?"

"There's a man—"

"You look stunning, by the way." She glanced from my head to my feet.

We had gone together to the hair salon, and she'd been with me when I bought the peacock blue sequined mid-length sheath dress, so I knew the compliment was related to the entire package.

"Thanks." Dixie was a stunning beauty who turned heads everywhere she went. At nearly six-feet tall, without the heels she was wearing tonight, she was thin with excellent skin and big Dolly Parton hair. I was a Midwestern transplant from Northwestern Indiana to Chattanooga, Tennessee, and often felt like a country hick compared to the beautifully made up and well-coifed women I saw walking the aisles of the local Publix grocery store. Dixie was a true Southern Belle, so a compliment from her went a long way to boost my confidence.

"Sorry for interrupting." She looked serious. "Tell me what's wrong?"

"There's a man at the front entrance making a scene." I leaned forward. "He looks homeless, but he brought his poodle."

Dixie shook her head. "Archibald Lowry."

I looked at my friend. "What?"

"Archibald Lowry. He never goes anywhere without his dog." She shook her head. "Remember, you went with me to his house a few weeks ago?"

I shook my head.

"No matter. I meant to warn you about him, but it totally slipped my mind with all of the preparations."

Dixie was the most organized person I knew, but she had been working like a maniac on this weekend fundraiser, so forgetting to mention a homeless man with a poodle would be attending the fundraiser was minuscule, all things considered.

"You've worked so hard organizing everything. I'm sure it will be great."

Dixie looked stricken. "Don't jinx me." She looked around.

I laughed. "Stop worrying. Everything has turned out beautifully. You should be so proud of yourself." I hugged her. "I know I am."

Dixie gave me a quick squeeze. "Thank you, but I won't be able to relax until this weekend is over."

We pulled apart. "Now, back to the homeless man."

Dixie chuckled. "He's far from homeless."

"Can you please talk to him? Linda Kay had to practically beg the board of directors to allow the fundraiser at the last minute and I don't want to get my boss in trouble."

When the ballroom for the Scenic City Hotel was flooded, and it looked as though the Poodle Rescue Association's annual fundraiser would have to be cancelled, I thought it would be a win-win to offer the Chattanooga Museum as an alternative location. The event would garner publicity and much needed funds for the museum and the poodle rescue would get to have the event that Dixie had spent so much time planning.

"Of course, I'll talk to Archibald." She marched toward the entrance with me by her side. "He's a cranky old windbag, but he's richer than Midas, so no one ever tells him 'no' about anything."

I stopped walking and Dixie turned to stare at me.

"Rich? I'm not sure we're talking about the same person."

Dixie laughed. "I'm sure we are. Let me guess, he's probably dressed in a tattered Scottish kilt that's too short and frayed on the bottom with socks that keep sliding down, a dingy white-ish shirt and black jacket that's probably older than I am with a scruffy beard and wild hair that looks like he hasn't combed it in the past decade."

"That's him." I stared at her in disbelief. "Is he Scottish?"

She chuckled. "A few years ago, Archibald Lowry paid someone to trace his family tree. That's when he learned about his Scottish roots. He claimed he was a descendant of some famous Scottish knight and started wearing a kilt to social functions."

"You don't mean Sir William Wallace, from the movie with Mel Gibson? *Braveheart*?"

Dixie nodded. "That's the one. He even went over to Scotland and bought a derelict castle, and had it renovated. He used to be just plain, Archie Lowry, but after his Scottish rebirth, he said his name was actually Archibald Leamhanach or something like that. He claims his ancestors' names were changed when they immigrated."

I gaped at her a few moments longer until she grabbed me by the arm. "He's a recluse who rarely comes out in public. That's why I went to his house to talk to him. He's a huge poodle fanatic and if you think my dogs are spoiled, you should see how he treats his dogs."

I paused for a moment as recognition dawned on me. "Is he the guy that lives out in the middle of the wilderness.

Dixie nodded. "Yeah, that's the one. He wanted to talk to me about including the poodle rescue in his will, but he had to *interview* me first." She used air quotes around interview. "It felt more like an interrogation, and I wasn't sure he intended to leave us anything. In fact, after a while I would have paid him money just to get out of there." She sighed. "I forgot I even invited him to the fundraiser. In fact, I think I promised him he'd be the guest of honor this weekend or something." She sighed. "I didn't think he'd really come. He rarely goes anywhere." She shrugged. "Oh well, come on. Let's get this over with before he blows a gasket."

When we got close to the lobby, we followed the raised voices to the area where a security guard who worked for the museum and Jacob Flemings, Linda Kay's assistant, were trying to quiet Archibald Lowry.

Jacob was in his early twenties and stylishly dressed, as usual, in a slim fitting tuxedo that reminded me of James Bond. His curly hair was slicked down and pulled back into a bun and his bright red rectangular glasses provided a touch of artistic flare. The only flaw in his meticulous look was the compression boot which he was forced to wear ever since he broke his ankle a month ago. To Jacob's credit, despite Archibald Lowry's blustering, he maintained his composure and kept a pleasant smile plastered on his face. But when he caught sight of me out of the corner of his eye, I noticed the strain on his face. His eyes pleaded with me for help.

Dixie turned on the southern charm and marched over to the kilted man. "Archibald, I'm so sorry I wasn't here to greet you." She leaned in, kissed his cheek and picked up the small silver poodle from the floor. "What an adorable poodle." She stared at it closely as I'd seen her do when judging dog shows. "This isn't Constantine."

Archibald Lowry stopped snarling at Jacob long enough to say, "Of course not." He swallowed hard. "Constantine died." He paused for a moment, sniffed and pulled a dirty handkerchief from his breast pocket. He blew his nose, wiped his eyes and then returned the piece of fabric to his breast pocket.

Jacob's eyes enlarged and he turned and limped away mumbling, "It looks like you have this under control, so I'll just go back to the party."

Dixie held the poodle to her chest and gave his owner a consolatory pat. "I'm so sorry."

Archibald coughed and nodded. "Yes, well. He was a good dog."

She held up the poodle. "Well, who is this handsome fella?" Archibald Lowry pushed his shoulders back and stood taller. "That is Constantine's son, Ildulb mac Causantin," he said proudly. "He was the son of Constantine the second."

Dixie cooed at the little poodle, "Now, Archibald, you know I can barely pronounce English, so there's no way I can wrap my southern tongue around all of that." She stopped cooing at the puppy long enough to flash a big smile at the puppy's owner. "Now, what's his call name?"

Unlike Dixie, I was relatively new to the dog world, but in my short indoctrination to the sport, I knew a call name was basically a nickname, what the owner called the dog, unlike the elaborate names the owners used to register their dogs with the kennel club. Those names were a mile long and usually included the name of the kennel where the dog was bred and some fancy name and any earned titles. The names were selected to amuse or impress when announced over the loudspeaker at big dog shows like Westminster or Crufts.

Archibald smiled smugly. "Indulf."

Dixie chuckled. "I supposed that's better than whatever you said the first time."

Just then, Indulf started to climb Dixie's shoulder, getting tangled in her hair.

I reached up and extracted the little poodle before he could cause any damage to Dixie's hair, earrings, dress or to himself.

Indulf was a tiny poodle, smaller than my six-pound poodle, Aggie. He was a smoky gray with soft eyes and long eyelashes. He looked up at me and my heart melted. I snuggled the little poodle close to my face and spoke baby gibberish for a few seconds until I realized I was being observed. I looked up and saw Archibald Lowry staring at me with a quizzical expression. The expression was logical considering we had yet to be introduced. "I'm so sorry. He's just so cute. I couldn't help myself."

"Where are my manners?" Dixie exclaimed. "Archibald Lowry, this is my best friend, Lilly Ann Echosby." She turned to me. "Lilly Ann, this is Archibald Lowry."

I extended a hand to shake, but Archibald Lowry ignored it. He leaned forward with both hands on his cane and inclined his head in a brief nod of acknowledgment.

I glanced down at Archibald's kilt and noticed it was held together with a gold pin shaped like a sword with a ruby stone in the hilt and an intricate design which included clear stones which glinted in the light.

"What a lovely…brooch." I stared at the stunning jeweled pin.

"It's called a kilt pin," he huffed.

"I'm sorry, I didn't—"

He sniffed. "Most Americans don't know the proper word to use."

"I'm so sorry, I didn't mean to offend you."

He took a deep breath. "Few Americans understand the history of the Scottish kilt."

I clutched the poodle to my chest.

Indulf licked my face and that small gesture softened something in Archibald Lowry's eyes. He looked at me, sighed and then launched into a lecture on the history of kilts.

"In the Scottish Highlands, dating back to the sixteenth century, kilts were the traditional dress for Gaelic men and boys."

He held up the elaborate pouch which hung from a chain around his waist. "Now, this is called a sporran." The top had a gold arch which was heavily engraved and studded with red jewels. He ran his hand along it. "This is the cantle." He moved his hand along the fur piece which extended downward. "This is Scottish goat hair, but I've also got them made from horse hair, rabbit and plain leather for less formal occasions." He continued to explain the history of the pouch and the kilt pin, which included a story of how Queen Victoria invented the kilt pin when she was inspecting Highland troops on a windy day and noticed a soldier struggling to keep the aprons of his kilt from flying up. He leaned close and chuckled. "True Scotsmen wear nothing under their kilts."

My mouth fell open and it took a nudge in the ribs from Dixie before I realized and closed it.

There was a moment of awkward silence and then Archibald Lowry laughed heartily. "I'm one of the wealthiest men in the country and people always ask me how I became so rich." He gazed at me. "Do you know what I tell them?"

I shook my head. "I haven't the foggiest idea."

"I tell them I acquired my money the same way everybody else has." He leaned forward so his mouth was within inches of my face. "I stole it."

The shock I felt must have been reflected on my face because he guffawed for several moments. He leaned forward again, as though he was about to say something, but stopped. His gaze was fixed over my shoulder and his face registered recognition.

I turned to see what had captured his attention but didn't see anyone I knew.

He scowled.

Dixie patted his arm. "Now, Archibald you're going to need to behave yourself and stop trying to shock my friends."

He laughed again, and then gave me a stiff bow. "Mrs. Echosby, it has been my pleasure meeting you, but if I can leave you with a word of warning: *Keep your friends close, and your enemies closer.*" He tapped the side of his head.

I forced a smile and remembered I was still holding his dog. I gave the poodle a final cuddle and ear scratch and then handed him back over to his owner.

Dixie grabbed Archibald by the arm and escorted him into the main room of the museum.

Just as I turned to follow, I noticed a strange man enter the reception. I probably wouldn't have noticed him, except he looked like he was watching Dixie but trying not to appear as if he was doing so. It wouldn't be unusual for a man to look more than once at Dixie. There's no question she was striking, but there was something about this stranger that sent a shiver up my spine. Suddenly, I sensed someone behind me, and I nearly jumped out of my skin. Turning, I saw my boyfriend. "Red, you startled me." I clutched at my racing heart.

He glanced into my eyes. "You really are scared. Sorry, I didn't mean to frighten you."

I took a deep breath. "I was looking at that man." I turned around to point him out, but he had vanished. "Well, he was here a minute ago." I glanced around.

"Should I be jealous that you're looking at other men?" Red joked.

I gave his arm a playful punch. "Don't be silly. I'm serious. There was this weird guy looking at Dixie and he gave me the creeps."

Instantly, his demeanor changed from playful flirting to serious, law enforcement mode. Red was stocky, but rock solid. He was five foot ten with dark eyes and sandy red hair which he wore in a cut which screamed former military. He still bore the scars, both internally and externally, from his years of service. The most visible was a scar across the right side of his face. The other scars were harder to see. Now he worked for the Tennessee Bureau of Investigations. Despite the fact that I found him to be a loveable teddy bear who could be extremely gentle and loved to cook, he could flip a switch and turn into a hard-nosed cop within seconds. I had seen the transformation before, in both Red and in my daughter's boyfriend, Joe Harrison, also former military and now a member of the Lighthouse Dunes, Indiana, police force. I can't put my finger on exactly what changes when the switch is flipped, but suddenly the air bristles with electricity and the hairs on the back of my neck stand up.

"Which guy? Can you point him out?"

We walked around the perimeter of the room, as inconspicuously as possible. I spotted Dixie talking to her husband Beau and Dr. Morgan, a short, bald man with an egg-shaped head that reminded me of the description of Agatha Christie's famous detective, Hercule Poirot. Dr. Morgan was the coroner and one of the members of Dixie's dog class. He was shy and socially awkward, but since Dixie had bought ten tickets at a hundred dollars per ticket for each of the members of the class she taught and gifted them to us, we felt it was our duty to come and support the fundraiser. What Dr. Morgan didn't know was that Dixie also hoped to hook him up with her socially awkward spinster cousin, whom she thought would be perfect for him. Needless to say, two socially awkward people in a crowded room was a pretty pitiful sight and Dr. Morgan looked as though he'd just as soon have a root canal as spend another second here.

We made two trips around the room and even ventured out to a few other areas of the museum, but I never saw the stranger again. We were just about to go back into the main reception area when I heard a yap and a dark gray fluff ball ran to me and took a flying leap of faith into my arms.

"My goodness, Indulf. What are you doing running around alone?" I whispered in the voice people only used with babies and pets. "If you went potty in the museum, Linda Kay will be furious."

Red reached over and scratched the poodle behind the ears. "Where did you meet this little guy and what did you call him?"

"Don't ask me to repeat it. I think it's Scottish." I petted the puppy. "He belongs to this eccentric old man named Archibald Lowry—"

Red stopped and stared at me. "Archibald Lowry? *The* Archibald Lowry?"

I stared at him. "You know him?"

He smiled. "Not personally, but I've certainly heard of him." He stopped and stared at me. "You don't?"

I shook my head. "Never heard of him until recently." I explained about the trip Dixie and I had made to his house. "Dixie drove the RV. I opted to stay in the luxury with the poodles." I shrugged. "Besides, I wasn't the one invited to meet with him."

"He's supposed to be one of the richest men in the South. I've never met him, but he's reported to be a recluse who rarely leaves his mansion unless it's to go to one of his other mansions."

I snuggled the poodle. "Well, this is his puppy." I looked around. "I don't see any messes anywhere. Do you?"

Red gave the area a quick glance and then shook his head. "Where is the mighty titan?"

I shrugged. "No idea." I looked down at the puppy and noticed he was licking one of his paws. A closer glance indicated a sticky red substance. "I think he's injured."

He examined the dog's paw and then his radar went up. "Take the dog and go back in the main room." The tone in his voice was complete law enforcement and left no room for argument.

I turned to obey and glanced back in time to see him reach for the gun he wore strapped to his side as he navigated around a corner.

A woman shrieked and Red raced in the direction of the scream.

I hesitated a half second and then turned back and followed him with the puppy clutched to my chest.

Around an alcove near a display of ancient swords, I saw a pair of white stubby legs, black socks which had fallen down around a pair of skinny ankles and a kilt which had hiked up during the fall to reveal that like a traditional Scot, Archibald Lowry wasn't wearing anything under his tartan.

Chapter 2

"My God, what happened?" Jacob whispered in my ear.

I hadn't even realized he was there until he spoke. I shook my head. "No idea."

Red squatted near the body and felt for a pulse. He stood up and pulled out his shield. "I'm going to need everyone to please go back into the main area and wait until the police arrive." He beckoned to Jacob. "I need you to get to Security and make sure every door is locked. No one leaves."

Jacob nodded, turned and hurried as quickly as a man in a heavy compression boot could, to take care of Red's request.

The crowd which had come in response to the scream, slowly returned to the main room.

A woman dressed in a short black dress was leaning against a pillar. From the way her hand was shaking, I knew she was the screamer.

I wanted to ask a million questions but Red held up his hand to forestall the barrage while he pulled out his cell phone. He called the police and reported the murder, indicating there was a TBI officer on the scene. When he was done, he turned to Dixie who had come to stand beside me. "Can you find Dr. Morgan?"

Like Jacob, Dixie looked dazed. After a few seconds, she nodded and stumbled away muttering under her breath. "*Death is my son-in-law, death is my heir.*"

Red frowned and glanced at me.

I smiled at the look of utter confusion on his face. "It's a quote from *Romeo and Juliet*." I inclined my head in Dixie's direction. "She quotes literature when she's nervous."

He raised an eyebrow but said nothing.

As much as I tried, I couldn't drag my eyes away from Archibald's rear. "It seems so undignified. Can you at least pull down his kilt, so he isn't so…exposed?" I whispered.

Red shook his head. "Sorry, but we can't touch anything. This is a crime scene, and everything must be left exactly as it's found."

In my head, I knew the red pool of blood I saw seeping under the body meant Archibald Lowry's death couldn't have been due to natural causes. However, my mind refused to grasp the fact that someone I was acquainted with, no matter how slightly, had just been violently murdered. "Are you sure it was murder?"

He nodded and walked over to the screamer.

I followed in time to hear him ask, "Can you tell me what happened?"

She looked up at Red and shook her head. "I came from the bathroom." She pointed a shaking finger in the direction of the ladies' room. "I saw him lying on the ground with all that blood." She turned even paler than she was before, a feat I wouldn't have thought physically possible. She clutched her hand to her mouth and ran to the ladies' room. She was thin and fit and made the sprint in four-inch heels, which elevated her athletic status considerably in my opinion.

Red looked like he was going to follow her, but that's when Dr. Morgan arrived. Red gave me a pleading look and inclined his head toward the ladies' room.

I nodded. Still clutching the poodle to my chest, I hurried to the restroom to check on the high heeled sprinter.

I halted inside the door. I could tell by the retching sound coming from one of the stalls that she'd made it in time. Motherhood had numbed me to practically every type of sickness involving bodily fluids. However, there was something about the sound of someone puking which caused me to shudder and want to plug my ears. I was ashamed to admit I stood as far away from that stall as the cramped confines of the restroom allowed. I turned on the water in the sink and pushed the button for the hand dryer, all in an attempt to blot out the noise. It didn't work.

She flushed the toilet and I pretended I was washing my hands. I stood at the sink with a toy poodle cupped between my chin and my neck. His claws gripped the top of my dress and he clung to my shoulder like a parrot. He was frightened and I could feel his little body shivering. I felt sorry for the poor little guy, but this dress had been a splurge. Dixie had driven me to Atlanta to a designer shop where there were belts that cost more than my monthly rent payment. However, when the clerk held up this dress, the heavens parted, angels sang, and I wept. When I saw the tag I wept more, but I still handed over my credit card. It had cost a small fortune, but it fit like a glove. The fabric felt like butter and floated on my hips like some type of fairy fabric. It was perfect and I knew if I hadn't gotten it, I'd regret it. I fully intended I'd someday be buried in this dress, so, while I was sad this cute little guy had lost his owner, he was going to need to come off. I didn't want to ruin a dress I paid a king's ransom for the very first time I'd worn it. I reached up and extracted him, taking care to avoid snags.

The sprinting screamer stumbled to the sink, turned on the tap and put her head down as close to the bowl as possible. She drank from the stream of water, then swished it around and spit. When she was done, she gripped the counter and stared at her reflection. "That was awful." She had a slight accent.

"I'm so sorry. Were you close to Archibald Lowry?"

A look of fright crossed her face but was quickly replaced with a smile that was more like a grimace. "What makes you ask that?" She forced a fake laugh.

"You found him and you seem really upset…" I tried to make my tone sound concerned rather than accusatory.

"Well, I didn't know him at all. I just happened upon a dead body." She fidgeted to turn off the faucets and remove all traces of her discomposure. "Stumbling across someone who's just been brutally beaten and stabbed would upset any *normal* person."

She emphasized normal as though to indicate that I wasn't. Previously, I felt compassion for her. However, that dried up quickly, especially as she glanced at me as though I was the hired help, which technically I was, but that wasn't the point.

"How did you know he'd been brutally beaten and stabbed?"

She took a tissue and patted at her face, but then glanced at my reflection in the mirror. "What?"

"He was lying on his stomach, face down. It was impossible to see his face, and you certainly couldn't have seen the wound." I wet a tissue and casually wiped the poodle's paws. "If you just stumbled across his dead body, how did you know he'd been brutally beaten and stabbed."

"In case you missed it, Nancy Drew, there was a rather large pool of blood beneath him. Anyone with common sense could see that he *must* have been stabbed."

Oh, it was on, now. "Nancy Drew was a teenager with a college boyfriend who played varsity sports. My boyfriend is that Tennessee Bureau of Investigations Officer out there and you'll have to work on your acting skills before you try that routine on him." If I hadn't been holding a poodle, I might have given her a neck roll and two finger snaps. Thankfully, Indulf prevented me from being more obnoxious.

After a long pause, she gave a nervous giggle. "I'm sorry. I didn't mean to be rude. It's just, well, I barely knew the man and I certainly don't want to get dragged into this nasty business simply because I stumbled across his body after he was murdered."

I lowered the eyebrow I'd raised and tried to look as neutral as possible.

She sighed. "I'm just scared. I mean, someone killed that man. If the killer thought I might have seen something, I could be in danger too."

The fact that it was the truth made this story much more powerful than the last performance she'd tried. She wasn't covered in blood and despite the four-inch heels, I doubted she could have plunged a knife or sword into Archibald Lowry's chest. He may not have been a young man, but he looked burly and was probably strong enough to have at least put up a fight. I didn't believe she killed him, but I still didn't like her. "Understandable, but what *did* you see?"

"Not much. I saw the man in the kilt arguing with someone. I couldn't tell who, because he was behind the pillar. The next thing I know, the other guy takes one of those weapons, bashes the old guy in the face and then plunges…" She took a deep breath and swallowed hard. "That's when I screamed and ran."

"Well, you didn't get far."

"No, I started to feel sick, so I looked around for a place to…well, you know." She waved her hand in a manner that made me ask.

"Where'd you get sick?"

"Large planter outside."

I'd have to remember to tell the cleaning crew.

"I'd just finished when I saw you two coming around the corner."

There was a knock on the door. "Lilly, are you okay?"

I walked to the door and opened it. "Yes, I'm fine." I held the door open so Red could enter.

He glanced around and, seeing that we were the only ones here, he walked inside. He turned to the screamer who was reapplying her lipstick. "Are you okay?"

She pursed her lips and then took a tissue and blotted the excess before responding. "Of course, it was just a shock."

He took out a notepad. "I'm Dennis Olson with the Tennessee Bureau of Investigations and I need to ask you a few questions."

She turned. "Of course, but as I was telling your girlfriend, I didn't know the man who was murdered."

Red glanced at me and I gave a slight shake of my head. "Well, let's start with your name."

She paused long enough for me to suspect that the name was a fabrication. "Fiona Darling." She reached into her bag and pulled out a business card, sauntered over to Red and handed it to him.

She stood so close that when she leaned back against the counter and flipped her thick red hair, it landed on Red's shoulder. It took every ounce of my willpower to keep from flipping it off.

Red seemed oblivious as he read her card. "Darling Detective Agency?"

"Yes, I'm a private investigator, although I'm not here tonight in any type of professional capacity." She flashed a smile which nearly blinded me.

I barely noticed her perfume when she was at the other side of the room, however, up close and personal, it was overpowering and caused my eyes to water.

"What did bring you here tonight?" Red asked.

She reached over and scratched Indulf behind the ear. Even though poodles are not known for being aggressive, I wouldn't have minded if he'd tried to amputate a finger or two. To my dismay, the little traitor merely wiggled and licked her hand.

"Aren't you cute." She leaned down and cooed.

Indulf missed another opportunity to show his loyalty and merely wiggled more and licked her hand.

She chuckled. "I just love dogs." She looked at me. "What kind is he?"

That set off mental alarms. "He's a poodle."

She colored, but tried to downplay her faux pas. "Well, of course he is."

Indulf redeemed himself when he sneezed in her face.

She froze for a few seconds, then took a tissue and patted her skin.

I gave Indulf an extra pat. "Good boy," I whispered.

"Miss Darling, can you tell me what you saw?" Red asked.

Fiona Darling related the same tale she'd told me, however this time she stressed that she hadn't seen the actual murderer. She fluttered her eyelashes and leaned in, keeping a hand on Red's arm much longer than I deemed necessary. I wasn't a jealous person, but Fiona Darling was an attractive woman, endowed with a couple of attributes which made her stand out. And she was certainly trying to use them to her advantage.

Red asked a few other questions, but then allowed the redheaded gumshoe to leave with a promise to make herself available for further questioning.

Her hips swayed far more than necessary as she sashayed out of the women's room. When she left, Red turned to me. "What do you think?"

"She wears too much perfume, she practically tossed herself at your feet and she wears way too much makeup. I don't like her. More importantly, what did you think?" I glanced at him. "She's an attractive woman."

"I didn't notice."

I stared at him, hand on hip. "Really? You didn't notice a tall, thin, redheaded bombshell with stunning blue eyes who flung her hair on your shoulder." I demonstrated the fling.

"Not my type."

"Really? What part exactly? Tall? Thin? Blue-eyed? Gorgeous? That's not your type? Are you seriously going to tell me you prefer...what? Short, fat—"

He hovered his hand over my head. "I prefer about...yay tall, dark haired and dark-eyes."

I suppressed a smiled. "Fat?"

He came even closer and put his arms around my waist. "I prefer curvaceous." He leaned down close to my ear. "With a razor-sharp mind, a generous heart and..." His lips grazed my ear.

"And?" I breathed hard.

"And, I prefer a woman who is intelligent enough to recognize a poodle when she sees one."

We kissed. After a few moments he repeated his question from earlier. "What did you think?"

"I think that was a good answer."

His lips twitched. "I meant about her story."

"She's hiding something."

He grinned. "Agreed." He pulled me close. "Jealous?"

"Of course not," I lied. "Should I be?"

He kissed me. "Absolutely not, but it would make me happy if you were."

There was something in his eyes that told me he was telling the truth. He kissed me again and I forgot about Fiona Darling. When we separated, he said, "I'm going to be here for quite a while. I can get one of the patrol cars to take you home—"

"I'm sure Dixie and Beau will make sure I get back to my house safely."

He nodded and started to speak, but the door opened. An older woman took a couple of steps inside but halted when she saw Red and I.

"Oh, I'm sorry. I—"

Red apologized and we both left.

He got stopped by one of the detectives, so I went in search of Dixie and Beau.

I spotted Jacob near one of the buffet tables with the other members of our dog class, B.J., Monica Jill and Dr. Morgan.

Bobbie Jean Thompson, B.J. to her friends, was a short, African American woman with dark skin and a big personality. "Girl, I knew you'd have the scoop. What's that fine looking TBI man of yours got to say about this mess?"

"He said he's going to be here awhile."

"You know what I mean. Does he know who did it?" B.J. asked.

"Not yet, but he just found the poor man."

B.J. shook her head. "Poor man my big toe. Archibald Lowry is one of the richest men in the state. They say when the government needs a loan, they call Archibald Lowry."

"Did you know him?" I asked.

"Pshaw." She snorted. "Archibald Lowry and I didn't mix in the same social circles." She stared down her nose at me and I laughed.

"I don't think Archibald Lowry mixed in anybody's social circle," Monica Jill whispered. Monica Jill Nelson was tall and thin with long dark hair and dark eyes. She was my realtor and had helped me find the house I was currently renting and hoping to soon buy.

"I can't believe someone was actually murdered." Jacob took a sip of champagne. "The board of directors is going to freak out."

"Did you call Linda Kay?" I asked.

Linda Kay Weyman was our boss. She was a kind-hearted woman who had gone to bat for me and convinced the board to allow the event to take place at the museum. I felt horrible thinking that doing a favor for me would cause her distress.

He nodded.

I sighed. "Maybe they'll accept my resignation in lieu of Linda Kay's head on a silver charger."

"You've worked here long enough to know Linda Kay will never stand for that." He blushed. "Bad choice of words."

Linda Kay ran the museum. Even though she only had one leg, she was certainly a force to be reckoned with. A southern lady with style and gentility, she had a spine of steel. I'd place money on Linda Kay in any fight she undertook. However, I certainly didn't intend for her to have to fight on my behalf. After all, Jacob was a permanent employee and I was merely a temp.

"Well, I don't intend for Linda Kay to take on the board of directors on my behalf," I said.

Jacob took another sip from his champagne. "She's already working on damage control."

"We can't have you losing your job over a murder you had nothing to do with." B.J. tossed back a glass of champagne. "I guess we'll just need to make this right."

I stared at her. "What are you talking about?"

"We'll just have to solve the murder." She looked at me. "And by we, I mean you." She gave me another stare. "If we catch the murderer, then the board won't be angry, and you keep your job."

"I can't find a murderer. Are you drunk?"

She grabbed another glass of champagne. "Not yet, but I'm working on it."

"Working on what?" Dixie joined our group.

I stared at my friend. "B.J.'s lost her mind."

"Honey, that's not the issue. I lost that a long time ago." She chugged back another glass of champagne. "This stuff is pretty good."

"Don't you dare get drunk and puke in a planter. We've already had one person do that tonight."

"Ughh." Jacob rolled his eyes and sipped his champagne. "I don't even want to know."

"I'm not drunk." She smiled. "Not yet anyway. However, I could use a few more glasses of this bubbly liquid courage."

"What are you all talking about?" Dixie asked.

"B.J. thinks I need to solve this murder."

Monica Jill picked up a glass of champagne. "B.J.'s not the only one."

"Et tu, Brute?"

"Et tu?" B.J. stared. "Was that some kind of sneeze?"

I chuckled. "It's from Shakespeare. It's what Julius Caesar said when he saw Brutus, the person he *thought* was his friend," I looked pointedly at Monica Jill, "was involved in the plot to murder him. It means, *You too, Brutus?*"

Monica Jill nodded. "Yep, me too."

I turned to Dixie. "They're all crazy. Maybe there's something in the champagne." I stared in my glass.

"What's so crazy about it?" Dixie looked at me. "It's not like this is your first rodeo."

I stared at her as though she'd lost her mind and then glanced at all of them. "I think you've all gone crazy." I reached over and took each of their glasses of champagne which was a challenge while cuddling a poodle who was trying to drink from the fluted glasses.

Dixie took the poodle.

"Thank you." I placed the fluted glasses down and turned back to my friends. "I'm not a detective and just because I got lucky a couple of times doesn't mean I plan to quit my day job and become Nancy Drew."

All three women and Jacob stared back at me.

Dixie turned to B.J. "In the words of Queen Gertrude from *Hamlet*, 'The lady doth protest too much, methinks.'"

"Uh huh." B.J. nodded. "Methinks so too."

"Yep, ditto," Monica Jill said.

I glanced at Jacob.

He raised an eyebrow. "Don't even look in my direction."

I picked up a glass of champagne from the table and downed it. This was going to be a challenge. "You've all lost your minds."

Chapter 3

Dixie and Beau drove me home. It was late or rather early Saturday morning when the police got everyone's names and addresses and allowed us to leave. However, I couldn't complain since Red had only gone as my date, and he was still there working and probably would be for several more hours.

By the time I got home, Aggie was curled up in a ball in the middle of my bed.

Aggie was the six-pound, black toy poodle I'd adopted before I left Indiana. My vet estimated her age at two years old. Surprisingly, she hadn't woken when I arrived, so I was able to watch her unimpeded for a few minutes. Her chest expanded as she slept, and I couldn't help smiling as I listened to her snore. An uninformed person, or non-dog owner, would think she'd worked hard based on how heavily she slept and the sound of her snoring. I glanced at the white fluff scattered around my bed. I saw the plastic squeaky that had once resided inside the white lamb toy, but was now outside with a hole that I suspected would match Aggie's teeth perfectly. Apparently, gutting stuffed animals, sleeping, eating and just being adorable was exhausting. I stared a bit longer and then bent down and caressed her muzzle. She opened her eyes and stared at me. Then, she gave my hand a lick. She was small, but she was such a big part of my life. I picked her up and carried her outside to take care of her business. I carried her partly because she was so cute and partly because since we'd moved, she preferred playing a game of catch me if you can instead of going outside and taking care of business. Dixie assured me I was playing into her paws every time I allowed the game to continue. My compromise was to carry her and place her outside rather than engaging in the sport.

Outside, Aggie shook, pranced around a bit and then quickly squatted and took care of business.

When she was done, I opened the door and she came inside, taking the time to stretch multiple times. Her life is so hard.

Despite my late arrival and the fact that it was Saturday and I didn't have to go to work, Aggie woke me up at six, as she always did. Feeling the weight of her walking up my body and standing on my chest, I rolled over to the side, forcing her to clamber off.

From my side position, I felt her breath on my face. When I opened my eyes, she was mere inches away.

"It's Saturday. I don't have to go to work and since I let you out to go potty about three hours ago, I doubt that you have to go potty now."

Aggie licked my face.

"Ugh." I sat up and wiped my face. "What have you been eating? Your breath smells awful." I stared at her.

Aggie wagged her tail in the way she had that made the bed shake. Then, she ran down the stairs I kept beside the bed to help her climb up and down.

Resistance was futile so I picked her up and went to the back door. I let Aggie out, locked the door and went to answer my own call of nature.

When I was done, I thought about climbing back in bed, but my cell phone vibrated on my nightstand and I realized sleep was over for today.

I picked up the phone and saw the face of my daughter, Stephanie, staring back at me. "You're up pretty early today. Aren't you on Central Time?"

Stephanie gasped. "I'm so sorry, Mom. I wasn't paying attention to the time. Lucky and I were just getting back from our walk and…I thought I'd call."

Lucky was a golden retriever she adopted after she found him injured and cowering under the deck at my last rental while she was visiting. He had been highly trained and was a great dog. However, something in her voice made me wonder if all was well. "Are you okay?"

"I'm fine." She sighed.

"How's work?" Stephanie was a successful attorney in Chicago. "Lucky? Joe?"

"Works fine and Lucky is wonderful. In fact, he's the best representative of his sex I know."

That narrowed down the problem. "I take it things aren't great between you and Joe?"

Joseph Harrison was a Lighthouse Dunes policeman and a member of the K-9 unit with his Plott Hound, Turbo. Stephanie and Joe started dating after he helped us figure out who murdered my estranged husband, Albert. They really seemed perfect for each other, although Lighthouse Dunes was just over an hour from Chicago, and I suspected the distance would become a problem at some point.

"Anything you want to talk about?" I asked tentatively. As her mother, I knew I was entering dangerous territory. Life as a parent was a delicate balance for both of us. Stephanie obviously wanted to talk, or she wouldn't have called at six in the morning. Yet, she didn't want to be the crybaby who ran to her mom when her problems got too much. I wanted to be there for my children but didn't want to overstep. I wished, not for the first time, that someone had created a manual for this.

"Not really."

I sighed. "Okay, so how's the weather in Chicago?"

"Why do men have to be so stubborn?"

For the next fifteen minutes, I held the phone while Stephanie poured out her heart. I listened but wasn't idle. I let Aggie inside, made coffee and started cooking bacon, eggs and toast. Stephanie needed to get things off her chest, but she didn't particularly need advice from me. When she was finished venting about Joe's faults, which basically amounted to his unwillingness to give up his job and move to Chicago, she sighed again. "What do you think I should do?"

"I think you should come visit your mother."

She paused. "No, what do you think I should do about Joe? Don't you think it's archaic and chauvinistic for him to expect me to give up my career and move to Lighthouse Dunes? I mean if he isn't even willing to entertain the idea of moving to Chicago, then what's the point of our continuing to see each other?"

I listened for another three minutes. By the time she finished talking, my breakfast was done. I took it outside and sat at the table on my deck. She paused. Unfortunately, the moment she chose for me to respond was the exact moment when I'd just shoveled bacon and toast in my mouth. I chewed quickly and gulped some of my coffee to help the lump slide down easier. "I'm serious. I think you and Lucky should come down to Chattanooga. A short vacation away from the situation might help you sort through your feelings and put things in perspective. Besides, you haven't seen the house I'm planning to buy, and I'd love to get your opinion about some of the changes I'm planning."

Stephanie hesitated for a few seconds. "I suppose Lucky and I could take a few days off. I don't have anything pressing at work and it might be good to be unavailable to certain people for a little while."

"Great."

We talked for a few minutes, but I could tell she had warmed up to the idea of a little getaway. By the time I finished my breakfast, she was already surfing the Internet for the best flights.

I looked down at Aggie. "Breakfast before seven on a Saturday. I hope you're happy."

She wagged her tail, oblivious to my sarcasm. She was happy that my attention was focused on her.

I showered, dressed and tidied up. Dixie was coming over later for day two of the fundraising activities which involved a trip to Archibald Lowry's estate for a poodle specialty and demonstrations from our dog club. The East Tennessee Dog Club Association would put on a show for agility, obedience and tracking. I gazed out in the yard at the open tunnel, closed tunnel and the PVC jumps Dixie gave me to practice with Aggie. Neither one of us were exactly sure about those, and so far all I've done is look at them while Aggie sniffed them. However, today wasn't the day for practicing.

"You have got to be joking? I can't adopt another dog. I can barely handle the one I've got!" I stared at my friend.

Dixie smiled. "You're looking at me like a dog looking at a new bowl."

"I'm not exactly sure what that means, but if you mean I'm looking at you as though you've suddenly lost control of all of your faculties, then *yes*. Yes, I am."

She merely grinned. Dixie sat in a chair on the back deck of my house. It was a beautiful spring day in Chattanooga. Seventy degrees at eight in the morning and the crepe myrtle, dogwood, Bradford pear, and crab apple trees the previous owner had planted around the perimeter of the large two-tiered deck were blooming along with bright red, coral and orange tulips, purple and white lilac bushes and white flowering Azaleas. The birds were singing and the sun shone bright. Sitting outside on my deck, the events of last night seemed like a dream. Surely, there wasn't anything as horrible as a murder on a day like today.

Dixie sneezed. "I love Chattanooga, but all of this pollen is driving me batty." She took a finger and wrote "pollen sucks" in the heavy layer of yellow film that covered nearly every flat surface, despite my best efforts to wipe it clean.

"Thankfully, I don't have allergies, but we didn't have anything like this in Indiana."

"The weather man said this was the worse pollen season we've had in two decades." She sneezed three times in rapid succession, jostling the small fur ball that had fallen asleep on her lap.

Aggie, my black toy poodle stood on her back legs and sniffed the furry little interloper that distracted attention away from her.

Dixie watched the interplay carefully. I noted she kept a firm arm around the puppy and a close eye on Aggie.

The bundle of fur sat up and looked at Aggie. His body shook with excitement and when Aggie brought her nose close enough, the shaking increased and a tiny pink tongue quickly licked her nose.

Satisfied the fur-ball posed no threat, Aggie sniffed, got back down on the ground and walked away.

Dixie smiled. "See, Aggie approves."

I looked down at Aggie who lay on the deck near my feet, licking the pollen off her paws.

I stared at Dixie. "Is pollen harmful to pets?"

She stared at Aggie. "I don't think it'll hurt her, but dogs can get allergies. Have her eyes been watering a lot?"

I shook my head.

"Have you noticed excessive scratching? Sneezing?"

"Nope."

She shrugged. "She's probably fine, but you should ask your vet. It can be hard to tell with dogs. Pollen can get on their fur and paws and be absorbed through their skins. Usually, they'll scratch more or have hotspots where they bite at one part of their skin."

Dixie wasn't a vet, but she was a dog trainer with tons of experience competing and judging dogs, so I trusted her judgment.

I made a mental note to check with my vet. "We have an appointment in two weeks, so I'll ask then." I looked down at Aggie who had rolled onto her side and was basking in a ray of sunlight that cascaded through the trees. I smiled and tried to recall what my life had been like prior to adopting this six-pound bundle of joy, but I couldn't. More importantly, I didn't want to. I turned my gaze to Dixie who was still holding Indulf.

"Did Archibald Lowry have any family? Maybe he made provision for someone to take his dog if anything happened." I looked at Dixie. "Is that a thing? Do people make provisions for their dogs?"

She nodded. "Absolutely, and you should figure out who you want to raise Aggie if something happens to you."

I stared down at Aggie sprawled out on the deck. Geez, who knew owning a dog would involve so many details. I suppose it was time to update my will. My daughter, Stephanie, was a lawyer and she'd updated my will after my husband died. However, that was nearly a year ago. Since both of my children were grown up with lives of their own, I hadn't thought much about guardianship. I certainly hadn't thought about it in relation to my dog.

"Technically, you would be fostering little Indulf. If it turns out that Archibald Lowry has family, or made arrangements for him, then you'd have to give him back." She paused and gazed out over the yard, but I could tell her mind was miles away.

I snapped my fingers. "Earth to Dixie."

She came back from whatever mental vacation she'd just taken. "I'm sorry. I was just thinking back to a conversation I had with Archibald when I visited him." She sighed. "I'm pretty sure he said he didn't have any family, which was why he was interrogating or interviewing, depending on how you look at it, me."

"I don't understand."

"If he had family, then he most likely would have left his money to them. If he didn't have a will, then that's what the court would do. They'd give the money to his relatives." She stared at me. "I'm almost positive he said he didn't have any relatives." She puffed out her chest and brandished a Scottish accent. "Last in the line of a distinguished lineage."

Dixie's southern drawl didn't lend itself to a Scottish accent, but she did an admirable job of imitating Archibald Lowry's mannerisms.

"Well, he was very wealthy and there's nothing like money to bring distant relations out of the woodwork."

Dixie frowned.

"What's wrong?"

She paused. "Did Red say if they had any ideas who could have done this?"

"I haven't talked to him. He sent me a text at around three this morning to let me know he made it home. He was going to grab a couple of hours of sleep and then head back to work."

Something in the way her hands fidgeted and her brow unfurled made me ask, "What's really bothering you?"

She paused. "Honestly, I don't really know. Something about the whole thing just feels wrong." I started to ask a question, but she halted me by raising her hand. "I know I'm not making any sense, but I just have this weird feeling that something's not right." She shuddered. "By the pricking of my thumbs, something wicked this way comes."

"Alright, now you're scaring me. I know you quote everything from the Bible and other great literature to *Hee Haw* when you're nervous, but in less than twenty-four hours, you've quoted *Hamlet*, *Romeo and Juliet*, *Macbeth* and *Julius Caesar.*"

She smiled. "Well, I did major in English Literature and technically, I believe you're the one who quoted *Julius Caesar.*"

"Stop splitting hairs.

She released a heavy sigh. "I know you don't want to get involved in another murder and I feel terrible asking you, but I was hoping you would reconsider and pull out your deer stalker one more time and look into who could have killed Archibald Lowry."

I stared at my friend for several seconds and collected my thoughts. "Let me start by saying, Okay, I'll do it." She started to thank me, but this time it was my turn to halt her. I held up a hand. "However, I just want to know, why? Why is this so important?"

Dixie took a deep breath. She looked down on Indulf and thought for a few seconds.

"You know how when you saw that poor woman murdered on that pet camera, you kept thinking how you would feel if someone saw Stephanie murdered? Well, I never had children." She smiled. "Not the kind with two legs anyway." She petted Indulf and sighed. "My parents are both dead and I spent a lot of time with older relatives, uncles, aunts and…well, I guess I've always had a soft spot in my heart for older people." She shrugged. "That's probably why I made sure Chyna and Leia were both registered therapy dogs." She glanced at me. "You know, we go into nursing homes once a month." She dropped her gaze. "Some of those older people would just break your heart, especially the ones who don't get visitors from family or friends. They're so happy to have someone to talk to, or a warm body to hug." She snuggled Indulf. "I think Archibald Lowry reminded me of those people." She shook her head. "I know it doesn't make any sense. The man was richer than almighty God. He could certainly afford to pay someone to spend time with him, but…"

I reached out and squeezed her hand. "I get it. Archibald Lowry was rich, but he still didn't have someone to care about him."

She nodded. Her eyes filled with tears.

"Don't you dare cry." I hugged my friend. "You'll get me started."

Indulf was caught in between us and wiggled until he was able to lick both of us. We pulled apart and laughed.

"Besides, I'm responsible for the fundraising for the Eastern Tennessee Poodle Association, and Archibald Lowry's murder is ruining our big weekend."

I laughed. "I guess murder can put a damper on a fundraiser."

"I sound horrible, I know, but it's such a worthwhile cause and this is our biggest event of the year. The funds for this event allow us to rescue poodles from puppy mills and pay for vet services. I was hoping we could raise enough money to pay for extra services which can really improve the quality of life for these dogs." She sighed. "I would love to create a fund where people who couldn't afford veterinary care could actually apply and get a grant to fund the services." She sighed.

Dixie's heart was as big as the state of Tennessee and when it came to poodles, her compassion was endless.

"Okay, well the weekend isn't over. We've got the poodle specialty this afternoon which should bring in quite a bit of money, right?"

She sighed. "I hope so. We've got a lot of poodles registered for the event. The entries have already been paid for and are nonrefundable, but we make quite a bit of money from visitors and concession sales."

"Then you're sure to make a fortune."

She stared at me.

"It's at Archibald Lowry's estate." I stared at her. "People will come out just to be nosy. I don't know how you convinced the hermit to let you host a trial on his secluded farm." I stared at my friend. "Are they still going to let you have the event there?"

She nodded. "I talked to his lawyer, first thing this morning. It's a good thing Archibald signed a contract. I think that's the only thing that prevented them from cancelling. I'm not sure it's still valid since he's dead, but they did agree to allow us to continue." She smiled shyly. "I promised we'd dedicate the trial in Archibald's memory, I'm going to make black arm bands for all of the competitors to wear and we're going to have a moment of silence."

"Well, that should have pleased them."

She nodded. "Archibald Lowry really did love poodles, so it is fitting."

Indulf sighed and snuggled down on her lap.

She handed him to me and pulled her notepad out of purse. "I need to swing by the store and pick up black fabric and scissors." She looked down at Indulf. "I should buy him a new collar."

I stared down at the rather gaudy collar he was wearing. It was black leather and looked as though it had been bejeweled. There were large rhinestones in red, clear, green and blue that went around the entire collar. "It does look a bit tacky."

"A bit?"

I shrugged. "I guess it goes with the name. I don't know that I can call him Indulf, though."

"What would you name him?" She glanced in my direction.

"Oh no you don't."

She gave me an innocent look. "I have no idea what you're talking about."

"You know if I name that dog then I'm going to get attached. I know your sinister games." I laughed.

"Well, then we'll just keep calling him Indulf."

I sighed and stared at the cute bundle of fur. "What about Rex?"

"Rex? That's Latin for king?"

I smiled. "I was thinking more along the lines of Rex Stout, author of the Nero Wolfe mysteries. I loved those books."

She smiled and gave the poodle a scratch. "Rex, it is."

I looked down into a pair of big dark eyes and my heart turned to liquid. "This is a bad idea," I said as I lifted the little gray fur ball and snuggled him close. "This is a very bad idea."

Chapter 4

Dixie's stop at the fabric store for black fabric expanded to include a visit to a major pet store. A couple hundred dollars later, I had purchased a crate large enough for both Rex and Aggie to stand up and turn around, but not big enough for them to use one side for sleeping and another for a toilet. Of course, no trip to a pet store was complete without a harness and leash for Rex, a new harness dress and treats for Aggie and more toys than a couple of poodles could gut in a month. I never dreamed I'd be the type of dog owner who enjoyed dressing my dog up in ridiculous costumes and outfits, but harness dresses were an entirely different matter. Dixie and my vet both recommended harnesses rather than connecting a leash to the dog's collar. Harnesses had a ring on the body that allowed me to hook the leash to my dog's back rather than her throat. That prevented pulling on her neck. Toy poodles don't pull a lot, which can pose a problem for more muscular dogs who pull and could damage their throat with a traditional collar and leash. However, I have yet to break Aggie of jumping on people. She was small and in no danger of overpowering anyone, however apart from the fact that it was bad manners, she had managed to get dirty paw prints on a cream-colored skirt and had ripped a couple of pairs of my hosiery. Harnesses helped control the jumping. The fact that manufacturers placed a tiny skirt on the harness just added to the overall cuteness factor. Aggie pranced around when she wore them, and it never failed to bring a smile to my face.

I told myself I wasn't buying things specifically for Rex. The larger crate and the male harness would be appropriate when I officially got a second dog. At least that's what I told myself. The reality was, Rex was already a part of my pack and if I had to give him back, I'd cry and be extremely sad.

However, until that day, I intended to enjoy each moment with him and not borrow trouble.

Archibald Lowry lived atop a mountain, but unlike Dixie's home on Lookout Mountain where there were houses, schools, restaurants and an entire community, Archibald Lowry's estate was on an extremely isolated area on Signal Mountain.

Dixie traversed the steep narrow roads with confidence and more speed than I would have deemed safe. However, she was familiar with mountain driving.

"Why would anyone want to live out in this wilderness?"

Dixie chuckled. "If you open your eyes and loosen your grip on that door handle, you'll see that it's really beautiful up here."

I opened one eye and quickly shut it. "I'll take your word for it."

"Honestly, this is a lot more rural than I would want, but if you like hunting, fishing and nature, it's amazing." She glanced in the rearview mirror.

I turned to my friend. "How much nature?"

She glanced in my direction. "Lots of nature. There are bear, wild boar, turkeys." She shrugged. "The other side of the mountain has a gated community with large three to ten acre lots. There are also bigger lots which are perfect for what they call *gentleman farms*. Archibald Lowry lived on the larger acreage. I heard he owned over a hundred and thirty acres of land."

"That had to have cost a small fortune. How did Archibald Lowry make his money?"

She glanced in her rearview mirror. "No one really knows for sure. He came out of nowhere. He dabbled in real estate, mining, importing and exporting, he bought and sold businesses, and pretty much did anything and everything."

"Seems strange to me."

Dixie glanced at me sideways as she navigated around a curve and adroitly avoided a fallen tree limb. "Why? Isn't it called diversifying when you've got your fingers in lots of pots?"

"No, I mean it's strange that there's not one thing he's known for." I paused for a minute to collect my thoughts. "I don't know that many truly wealthy people. However, if you think about some of the richest people in the country, you can pretty much tell what they did to get their money. Oprah Winfrey was in entertainment, Bill Gates was in software, Warren Buffett invested in the stock market, Sam Walton was in retail."

Dixie looked in her rearview mirror again. "I see what you mean. Well, I'm sure someone knows for sure how he made his money, but it's not me."

"Why do you keep looking back in the mirror." I glanced at my side mirror and noticed a car further back with its daylight running lights on, but it wasn't close enough to notice any other details.

"That car has been behind us for quite some time."

I turned to look out of the back window. However, I couldn't see much. "Do you think they're following us?"

Dixie glanced back quickly and then shrugged. "Maybe they are. I mean, it could just be someone doing the same thing we're doing, following the signs to the dog show."

"Then why do you seem nervous?"

She hesitated and then shivered. "I don't know. I just feel like someone walked over my grave."

I stared at her and then glanced in the mirror again. "Shakespeare?"

"*To Kill A Mockingbird*." She saw my nervousness and chuckled. "It's just an old saying the old folks used to say when they got a chill."

"Do you think I should call Red?" I reached down and grabbed my cell phone from my purse.

She shook her head. "Let the poor man sleep. I'm sure it's nothing."

We both tried to shake off the uneasy feeling, but I noticed Dixie glancing in her mirror more than usual and I caught myself looking back several times before we arrived at the show site.

Dixie followed several handmade signs that directed us to the Poodle Specialty Show. Eventually, she pulled up to the area where the events were to be held.

There was a flat area where cars, RVs and trailers were parked. There was also a large tent with grooming tables holding all varieties of poodles: toys, miniatures and standards in white, black, brown, and gray. Practically every solid color was represented.

Since reconnecting with my college friend, I had learned a lot about dogs in general, and specifically poodles, and dog shows. Dixie owned two standard poodles, Champion Chyna 9th Wonder of the World and Grand Champion Galactic Imperial Resistance Leader, also known as Leia. Chyna and Leia were retired obedience, agility and conformation champions. However, Dixie brought them out for events like this weekend where they could demonstrate their skills. Aggie was here merely to observe and, hopefully, learn how to behave like a trained poodle by hanging around with other trained poodles. Rex was here relaxing.

A poodle Specialty meant the only dogs entered would be poodles, so I wasn't surprised at the number of poodles present. From the smallest toy poodles like Aggie and Rex, to the largest standard poodles this event was a poodle lovers' dream, and ever since Aggie came into my life, I had become a lover. Although, just like Dixie, I liked dogs of all kinds. I loved my daughter, Stephanie's golden retriever, Lucky, and her boyfriend, Joe's Plott Hound, Turbo. I was quite fond of the dogs from our dog club, too. Dr. Morgan's German shepherd, Max, B.J.'s Westie, Snoball, and Monica Jill's dog, Jac, whom she lovingly referred to as a mutt.

I walked through the grounds and admired all of the dogs and marveled that less than a year ago there were no dogs in my life. My husband, Albert, didn't like them. When Albert dumped me for a woman younger than our children, I realized she'd done me a favor. I was able to do the things that I enjoyed, including owning a dog. I moved from Indiana to Chattanooga, which I loved, and I had friends and was putting down roots.

"What are you grinning about?" Dixie glanced at me.

"I was just thinking how different my life is now."

She gave my shoulder a squeeze and we walked our pack to the main tent.

Dixie had corralled a number of folks from the Eastern Tennessee Dog Club to help, even though they weren't technically members of the Poodle Association, so I saw quite a few familiar faces. Beau, Dixie's husband, was one of them.

"Great, there's Beau." Dixie pointed toward the area near the side of the tent with a large dog pen, several stadium chairs and refreshments for both humans and canines. "He's got our crates set up."

"Thanks, dear." Dixie kissed Beau's cheek as he took the standard poodles from Dixie, freeing her hands.

He removed the leashes and put the larger dogs in their crates. "You've got me trained pretty well," he joked.

She smiled. "It only took a quarter of a century to do it."

Chyna and Leia were great with Aggie and all dogs, but I knew they were going to be participating in some of the demonstrations later and didn't need to be aggravated with a playful puppy, so I unloaded the new crate I'd bought and placed Aggie and Rex inside. Aggie wasn't crazy about not being with the big dogs and voiced her displeasure.

"She's so loud and disruptive, what am I going to do?" I asked Dixie.

She picked up a blanket laying across the arm of one of the chairs and placed it over the small dog crate. Similar to covering a squawking bird, the cover immediately quieted the angry poodle.

I stared at my friend. "You're a genius."

She shook her head. "Not even close, but this isn't my first rodeo. You should have heard Chyna when she was a puppy."

Beau shook his head. "She *screamed* whenever Dixie took Leia out and left her behind."

Dixie left to talk to the volunteers who were working the trial. As one of the judges, she had some duties but was only judging a small group of puppies so she could participate in the obedience demonstrations later. Tomorrow, she'd take a more active role.

Beau and I sat and watched. The tent was sectioned into three major areas and each area was a ring with different poodles being judged. Dixie's puppy group was first and there were multiple fluff balls, all groomed to perfection, prancing around the ring as though they owned it. Dixie examined each one from head to tail and quickly pronounced a beautiful gray poodle the winner.

I passed several hours comfortably with Beau. We watched the trials and killed time by trying to guess the winners. Beau was right more often than I, but he'd spent a lot more years in this world than I had. Eventually, Dixie returned.

"I'm so hungry I could eat a horse," she announced.

Beau slid a cooler from behind his chair and opened it to reveal sandwiches, salads, and small containers filled with the jerky Dixie used to entice her dogs to perform to their highest levels. She called it, 'food they'd sell their souls for.' There was also a good supply of bottled water and cans of Diet Coke.

"I need to use the facilities, but…" I glanced around.

Dixie understood my revulsion of portable potties and smiled. "We'll go to the RV and take care of business and then we'll come back and eat." She turned to Beau. "Why don't you see if the dogs need to go potty."

Beau looked around for the leashes. "I'm not sure I'm up for task of taking four at once." He turned to Dixie. "Do you think they'll be—"

Dixie waved her hand. "Of course. They'll be fine. Just take them two at a time."

He nodded and took the two standard poodles first. Chyna and Leia were so well-behaved, they didn't need to be leashed, but I learned from Dixie that all dogs had to be leashed on the grounds of a dog show.

Dixie and I walked the short distance to the RV and took care of business. We were just on our way back when we heard a huge commotion.

"STOP!" I recognized Beau's voice and we ran toward it.

Just as a mother will recognize her child's cry in a room full of babies, I recognized Aggie's bark. My children called it my mom "Spidey sense." She had several different barks and while I hadn't figured out what they all meant yet, I knew this one wasn't good. There was a growl in between each bark that made the hair on my arms stand up. "Oh my God, Aggie!"

Chapter 5

We ran through the crowd. Just as we turned the corner, I saw a figure dressed in black pants, a black hoodie with a baseball cap and sunglasses racing across the grounds. I knew from experience that Aggie had issues with men wearing baseball caps, but there was a lot more going on here. The figure was running, and Aggie was pouncing and nipping at his pant legs, her leash trailing behind.

I rushed toward the fray screaming, "Aggie, no!"

Just as I got within fifty feet, I noticed that the figure dressed in black was also holding a small gray poodle.

I stopped and pointed. "He's got Rex."

At that moment, the figure turned toward us and saw me pointing. That's when Aggie leapt into the air like a guided missile and sunk her teeth into the man's arm.

He screamed and dropped his arm to his side with Aggie still attached to the fabric. In the commotion of trying to dislodge Aggie's teeth from his sleeve, he dropped Rex who fell to the ground. The poodle rolled a couple of times but then stood up and shook himself and then turned to add his bark to the fight.

The man gave his arm a vigorous shake and Aggie lost her grip on his sleeve and flew through the air.

"You get Aggie. I'll get Rex." Dixie ordered.

The man took off running full steam ahead dodging poodles, grooming tables and crowds of people. He rushed through the parking lot and jumped into a black pickup truck.

Aggie followed in hot pursuit. She lunged at the door of the truck, but the stranger managed to get inside. He quickly started the ignition with Aggie still barking and jumping at the truck's door.

The stranger gunned the engine, spinning dirt, pebbles and grass from his tires as he took off.

My heart pounded as I watched Aggie getting sprayed by the debris and still racing after her prey.

From the edge of the parking lot, I screamed, "Aggie, come!"

To my complete and utter surprise, she stopped, turned to look at me and then ran toward me full steam. From five feet away, she took a flying leap into my arms.

I reached out and caught her and then held her tightly to my chest.

Dixie ran up to me with Rex clutched in her arms. "That little poodle is fearless." She stared at Aggie.

I snuggled Aggie close. "I can't believe she actually came when I called." I turned to Dixie. "I'm so happy, I could cry."

* * * *

For over an hour I sat in Dixie's RV clutching Aggie to my chest. When Red arrived, he literally had to pry her out of my arms. It was only then that I realized I was shaking.

He pulled me to my feet, drew me close and held me tightly until the shaking stopped. I held onto him and cried.

"I'll be in the tent if you need me." Dixie slipped out of the RV.

I cried for what felt like hours. When I didn't have any more tears, I pushed away.

"I'm sorry."

Red lifted my chin, forcing me to look him in the eyes. "You don't have to apologize to me for being human."

I hiccupped. "How about for ruining your shirt." I pointed to where I had gotten makeup on his white shirt. I looked around for my purse. "I'm sure I have a wipe or a pen here that will get that stain—"

He gave me a gentle shake. "Lilly, I don't care about the shirt. I care about you." He glanced down at me. "Are you okay?"

I nodded. "I'm fine…now."

"Can you tell me what happened?" He looked around with surprise. "What?"

"Nothing, it's just…this is a really nice RV."

I realized he'd seen Dixie's RV many times, but this was his first time inside. I smiled. "Want the guided tour?"

He shook his head. "Maybe later." He directed me toward a surprisingly comfortable sofa and mumbled, "Might need a GPS to find my way out."

I smiled and sat. Aggie hopped onto my lap.

I petted her absently and recapped what happened.

He asked several questions which I felt like I should know the answer to. 'Did I get a good look at the person? Was I certain it was a man? How tall was he or she? Had I ever seen him or her before?' On and on the questions came until I wasn't sure about anything, other than the fact that I was tired.

He looked down at Rex. "Are poodles valuable?"

I shrugged. "You'll need to ask Dixie. She's the expert, but I do know that some champions can be worth several thousand dollars."

His eyes widened. "For a dog?"

I nodded, then reached into my purse and pulled out my cell phone and dialed Dixie's cell.

When she picked up, I asked, "Are you busy?"

She wasn't and said she'd be there shortly.

After a few minutes, there was a knock on the door and Dixie climbed inside.

Red asked her the same questions he'd already asked me, and her answers were much the same as mine. We were both more focused on the dogs than on the person who'd just tried to steal them. When Red asked Dixie about the value of the dogs, she confirmed what I'd said.

Red shook his head. "Is there a market for the dogs? I mean, if someone were to steal one of these dogs, would they be able to sell it?"

Dixie went into teaching mode. "Not really, not like stealing a valuable painting or a piece of jewelry. You can't just sell them to a collector. Like champion racehorses, the value is in the lineage and stud fees. If you have a champion that comes from a long line of champions, then you can sell the stud fees." She shrugged. "But you couldn't show the dog because you'd need the papers from the kennel registry." She sighed and got quiet.

"What?" Red asked.

Dixie took a deep breath. "I've been thinking about this a lot and it doesn't make any sense. I mean, why take Rex? You can't do anything without the papers from the American Kennel Club. No one is going to breed the dog without the AKC papers proving lineage and ownership. Besides, most responsible dog owners have their dogs microchipped or tattooed."

"I've heard of that with racehorses," Red said.

She nodded. "Exactly, most dogs," she waved her hand to indicate Aggie, "are not only tattooed and microchipped, but now they have tracking devices built into their collars." She picked up Rex who was sprawled out on the floor. She pointed to a small rectangular disc that appeared to be part of his collar.

I stared closely. "Is that what that is? I thought it was just part of the gaudy baubles on his collar."

Dixie shook her head. "It's a GPS tracking device."

Red stared. "So, if he had managed to get away with the dog, you could have tracked him like OnStar in a car?"

She nodded. "Exactly."

"I need to get one of those for Aggie."

She smiled. "They used to be pretty pricey, but now they're very affordable. You need the app on your cell phone, but they are great for locating lost pets. I haven't bothered with Chyna or Leia because they're both so well-behaved and obedient that I don't worry about them running off." She shivered. "I've never felt unsafe at dog shows before today. It's such a small, tight-knit community that I never bothered. However, I think I'll be purchasing trackers for both of my dogs." She glanced down at Aggie. "I don't think you need to worry about that little dog. She's a scrappy little thing."

I looked down at Aggie who was curled up in a ball on my lap and smiled.

We talked a bit longer but neither Dixie nor I had any additional insight into who might want to steal Rex or why. Eventually, Red left to question some of the people from nearby campers and RVs to see if they knew anything that would help him track down our poodle napper.

Beau brought in Chyna and Leia and we left the dogs locked inside the RV for the remainder of the day. Considering Dixie's RV was more luxurious than most people's houses, it wasn't a punishment. The dogs were all fine playing, chewing on digestible bones, and sleeping in the air-conditioned luxury.

Dixie and Beau had both driven separately, so he followed her home while Aggie, Rex and I rode with Red.

In a vehicle smaller than a 747, the drive down the mountain didn't seem quite as perilous as it had when riding with Dixie. Nevertheless, I was extremely happy to be back on the relatively level ground of Chattanooga.

Rex offered to take me to dinner, but I was worn out and opted instead for a pizza which we picked up and ate at my house.

"How are you and Stevie doing?"

Stevie was 'Steve Austin,' a Pitbull/Labrador mix that had adopted Red. The dog seemed vicious in the beginning, but had proven to be a real pussycat. He and Aggie became friends at first sight. I was always surprised at how gentle the big dog was with her whenever they played.

"I'm fine, although he's going to need reform school. He's got a problem." He leaned closely and whispered, "He likes to steal things. If you turn your back for more than two minutes, he'll nab something and then head downstairs where he collects the stuff. When I confront him, he just lays down on top of it and looks up at me like, *What? I have no idea how your underwear and socks got here.*"

I smiled. "Aggie used to do that. Dixie said it's because it has your scent on it."

He stared. "Why would he need to do that?"

"It makes him feel close to you." I smiled. "He's bonded to you and he misses you."

"That's weird."

I gave him a playful punch. "No, it's not. It's cute. He misses you. Haven't you ever worn something that belonged to someone you cared about because it had their scent on it and made you feel close to them?"

His lips twitched. "I suppose so, but Steve doesn't strike me as particularly sentimental, especially considering he likes to drink from the toilet and enjoys licking himself in front of company."

I laughed. "Just because he's uninhibited doesn't mean he isn't sentimental."

We finished eating and then Red stretched and prepared to leave. We lingered over our goodbyes and when we came up for air, he searched my eyes. "Are you sure you're okay? I can stay if you need me to?"

I glanced down at Aggie who was doing a full body stretch that looked like a complicated yoga position. "I'll be fine. I've got my watch poodles."

He reached down and picked up Aggie. "She is certainly a fierce little dog." He held Aggie so she faced him. "Don't ever let anyone tell you you're not a big dog."

Aggie licked his nose.

Red left and I locked the door after him. I tidied up the kitchen, tossed the pizza box, and put the remains of the wine in the fridge. I was just about to let the dogs out when my cell phone rang. One glance showed me the caller was Red.

"Did you forget something?"

"Don't forget to turn on your alarm system."

I smiled. "I will, just as soon as Aggie and Rex finish going potty."

We chatted a bit longer about nothing important, but the conversation left my cheeks feeling warm and a smile on my face. When the dogs were done, I let them in, engaged the alarm and headed to my bedroom.

I took a long bath and prepared for bed. By the time I was done, Rex and Aggie were curled up on my bed. I picked them up and moved them to their crate. Rex seemed fine with the arrangement but Aggie, who was accustomed to sleeping with me, wasn't happy.

"I'm sorry, girl, but you need to keep your brother company. He can't be trusted in the bed yet."

Aggie made her displeasure known for quite some time, but I turned on the television and settled down with my iPad to kill some time before I fell asleep. That's when I realized that in all of the confusion, I hadn't checked my emails all day. I had one from Stephanie with an itinerary for a flight to Chattanooga. I glanced at the times and realized her flight was scheduled to land in fifteen minutes.

I rushed to throw on a pair of yoga pants and a T-shirt on top of my nightshirt, slipped on a pair of tennis shoes, and to Aggie's delight, I opened the crate and released the poodles. "Come on, we're going to the airport."

Fortunately, I lived close to the airport. By the time I arrived, Stephanie was just coming out with her suitcase and her golden retriever, Lucky.

"Perfect timing." She hugged me while Lucky relieved himself at the curb and then stood on his hind legs and looked through the glass of the rear window at Aggie who was barking and pawing at the window, excited to see her friend.

We loaded her luggage into the rear of my SUV, opened the back door and allowed Lucky to jump in and reunite with Aggie.

"I'm glad to see you, but I almost missed your email."

Stephanie sighed. "I needed to get away. I needed to think."

"Does Joe know where you are?" I asked hesitantly.

She shook her head. "I told him we needed to take a break, but I didn't tell him I was coming here." She kept her face turned away so I couldn't see her, but her voice sounded tired.

"I'm sorry you two are going through a rough patch, but I'm glad you're here." I kept up a light-hearted commentary for the short trip home.

I pulled into the garage, opened the door to let the dogs out and helped Stephanie get her luggage.

Rex was excited about meeting Lucky and ran in circles.

Stephanie stared. "Who's this little guy?"

"Oh, I haven't told you about Rex." I scooped him up and headed up the stairs to unlock the door. "Come inside and we'll have some coffee and I'll introduce you properly."

I forgot to disarm the alarm and after a few moments, it went off. My hands were full with luggage and Rex and I yelled to Stephanie, "Can you disarm that for me? The code is your birthday month and year, and then press disarm."

Stephanie entered the code and the noise stopped. I took the dogs to the back door and put them all outside to allow Stephanie and me a few minutes of breathing space.

She glanced up at the vaulted ceiling. It was contemporary with angles and details that had been popular in the seventies and eighties. "Very modern."

"You don't like it?" I asked tentatively.

She shook her head. "No, I do like it. I saw the pictures you sent and the video that David took when he was here, but I had no idea how tall the ceilings really were." She paused. "It's just so different from the house you had in Lighthouse Dunes."

I nodded. "Exactly. I never really liked that house. That was your father's idea." I took a deep breath. "This house isn't large, and I know it needs updating, but I really like how all of the houses are different and the neighborhood has duplexes and single-family homes as well as townhouses. It's not a subdivision so there are no rules about what I can and can't do to my property."

She walked over and gave me a big squeeze. "Mom, I love it. I think it's perfect."

I released a breath and hugged her back. "Thank you, dear."

We put her luggage in the guest bedroom and then went to the back door.

"This is probably my most favorite part of the entire house." I opened the door and flipped on the lights so she could see the expansive, fenced in yard. The dogs were enjoying a game of chase. Eventually, they sniffed around and took care of nature's call. Then, they joined us at the table.

"This is surprising. It's in the city, but it's so private." Stephanie sighed.

"In the morning, we'll take a quick tour of the neighborhood."

She hugged me again. "I can see you're very happy."

"I really love living in Chattanooga."

She paused and then asked, "Weren't you scared moving so far away from everything you know?"

"I was at first, but...did I ever tell you about Miss Florrie?"

Chapter 6

Stephanie and I stayed up late into the night talking and getting caught up on the day-to-day mundane details you don't mention in a casual long-distance conversation. She was quiet when it came to talking about her relationship with Joe, so I shared how Rex came to be living with me and the excitement we'd had earlier in the day.

"Wow! What a day."

"You must be tired after your flight." I showed her where the supply of extra linens, towels and toiletries were and left her to prepare for bed. Since I'd already gone to bed once, my preparations were short.

Rather than crating the dogs, I pulled out a large dog bed and let Aggie and Rex cuddle together. They were asleep quickly and I quietly climbed into bed, hoping not to wake them. I'd deal with any cleanup from the puppy in the morning.

I turned the television on and prepared to fall asleep to a rerun of *Murder, She Wrote*, when I heard a light knock at my door.

"Mom?"

"Come in, dear."

Stephanie, wearing a T-shirt and shorts, entered followed by Lucky. "Mind if I join you?"

"Of course not."

She climbed in the bed and Lucky, ever the gentleman, waited patiently until I patted the bed. Then he jumped up and made three circles before finally settling down at Stephanie's feet and resting his head on her leg while looking up at her with such love, that I couldn't help but smile.

She reached down and gave him a gentle caress. "Every time I look at him, I think how lucky I am to have him in my life."

I glanced over at Aggie and Rex who were curled up together in their dog bed. "I know the feeling."

After a few minutes, she opened up about her relationship with Joe.

I listened quietly and patiently and silently prayed that I would know the right words to provide comfort, guidance or whatever she needed.

The clue to the underlying problem wasn't in the words she shared, but more in the silences and the slips that gave me insight into the real crux of the matter. When she had poured out her heart, I took a deep breath. "Honey, I wish I could tell you what to do, but I can't. What I can tell you is that you aren't me and Joe isn't your father."

She looked up. "I didn't mean—"

I waved a hand to stem the flow of apologies. "I gave up my career as a CPA because I wanted to." I sighed. "Sure, your father didn't want me to work, but ultimately, I *chose* to quit and stay home and raise you and your brother and to be a housewife. I can't blame your father for that, and I don't regret the choice I made." I smiled, realizing the truth behind the words. "If you want to continue your career, then I think you should. This is a completely different time that we live in now. Women today don't have to make the choices that we did twenty-five years ago. Also, just because my marriage to your father didn't last, doesn't mean that's what will happen to you and Joe."

"Mom, I know relationships are about compromise and I'm willing to make my share, but I don't see why I should be the one to have to give up the most."

I smiled. "Honey, remember when I was telling you about meeting Miss Florrie on the train and how she helped me realize that I was holding onto the memory of what my marriage had been, rather than facing the fact that my marriage had ended long ago? Well, it was that conversation that helped me to let go of the past and the hurt and to move forward and look for my 'happy place.'"

She smiled. "I remember when you told me you wanted to sell the house and move to Chattanooga. At first I thought you were crazy, but you looked so happy." She looked around. "Now, look at you. You moved six hundred miles away, you have two dogs and you're involved in a new relationship."

I smiled at the thought of my new life.

"You've found your happy place, haven't you?"

I thought for a moment. "Yeah, I think I have." I turned to look at my daughter. "Now, it's your turn. You have to decide what you want. You have to figure out what will make you happy. Do you want to continue living and practicing law in Chicago? Or, do you want to move back to Lighthouse Dunes? Or, maybe there's another option?"

She looked up at me. "What other option?"

"I don't know. Maybe, there's some place in between Lighthouse Dunes and Chicago where you can both be happy." I shrugged. "The world is wide open. You two are young and you can go anywhere you want. You could move to New Zealand or Paris or...anywhere."

She smiled. "I could get used to the warm weather here."

I smiled. "It didn't take me long to adapt to warmer weather." I sighed. "I guess, my point is once you decide what will make you happy, then you owe it to yourself to at least try."

"What if we chuck our jobs and move to Paris and we hate it?"

I smiled.

"What?" Stephanie asked.

"I was thinking about how I asked Miss Florrie almost that exact question."

"What did she say?"

"Well, Miss Florrie wanted to move to Chattanooga and open a restaurant." I smiled. "When I asked her what she would do if she moved to Chattanooga and she didn't like it, she laughed and said, *'Baby, that's easy. I'd keep trying until I find my happy place.'*" I smiled at Stephanie. "So, I'm going to tell you the same thing. If you moved to Paris or New Zealand and you didn't like it, then you could always come back or move someplace else. Moving doesn't have to be permanent."

She snuggled close to me and closed her eyes. "I guess I'll just have to figure out what will make me the happiest."

I kissed her forehead, turned off the television and went to sleep.

A few hours later, my alarm went off which started a round of barking that was loud enough to wake the dead. I picked up the poodles, thankful that Rex had managed to sleep through the night without an accident and called Lucky to follow. I went to the back door and let all of the dogs out, and then hurried to take a quick shower and get dressed for the final day of the Poodle Specialty and fundraiser.

One of the things I liked best about my neighborhood was the peaceful, remote feel of the street, but its close proximity to the city and amenities. Two blocks from my house was a post office and small shopping plaza with a yogurt shop, barber and pizza parlor. There were sidewalks, street lights, mature trees and lots of kids riding bikes and playing, all of which I deemed a positive. It was this proximity to what I deemed, *civilization*, that made me feel safe. I know some people, like my realtor Monica Jill, preferred living in the country with no neighbors and miles of farmland with cows, chickens and llamas. However, I found that isolation much more terrifying than any city street.

I stepped out of the shower and was surprised to hear a cacophony of noise. I recognized Rex's yap and Aggie's growling bark along with a much lower more guttural sound which I assumed came from Lucky.

I quickly put on my robe, grabbed my phone and ran to the back door. I made it at almost the same time as Stephanie. We rushed outside in time to see Lucky pounce on a figure in black and roll him to the ground.

The man screamed as Lucky bared his teeth and went for the man's throat.

Stephanie screamed, "Lucky, no!"

Lucky halted but kept his gaze fixed on his prey, teeth bared, and even from twenty feet away, I could hear the growl rumbling from his belly.

I looked around for Aggie who I expected to see in the heat of the battle. However, I was surprised to see her racing in circles around Rex. As I watched, I noticed that she was cutting her circles closer and closer, forcing the puppy further and further away from the fray.

"I don't know who you are, but this is private property," I yelled. "What are you doing here?"

I could hear the shaking in his voice. "Call off your dog."

Stephanie glanced at me and I nodded. "Lucky, come."

The golden backed up slowly, never removing his gaze from the man.

Once the dog was far enough away for comfort, the man released a breath and climbed to his feet.

Aggie herded Rex back to the deck so I was able to scoop both him and Aggie up in my arms. Once I knew the poodles were safe, I took a deep breath. "Now, who are you and what are you doing here?"

The stranger took this opportunity to make a mad dash for the fence. Lucky took off after him, but the stranger made it in time and slammed the gate closed behind him. Within a few seconds, I heard a motor and tires racing off.

Stephanie called Lucky and he trotted to her. She bent down and petted him. "Good boy." She turned to me. "What was that about?"

I shook my head. "I have no idea, but I better call Red." I dialed his number.

He bombarded me with questions, starting with, "Was it the same guy from yesterday?"

"I don't know."

"Did you have the alarm on? How did he know where you lived? What did he want?"

"No, the security system wasn't on because I'd just let the dogs out to go potty. I don't know if it was the same guy, so I don't know how he knew where I lived. And I have no idea what he wanted." I sighed. "Look, I haven't had coffee today so if you ask any more questions, I'm likely to bite you."

He chuckled. "I'm sorry, but I want to make sure you're safe. Since you won't let me give you one of my guns—"

"Absolutely not. I don't like guns and I don't want one."

"Alright, alright." Even though I couldn't see him, I knew he was holding up his hands in surrender. "Maybe I should stay there a few days, at least until we get to the bottom of what's going on."

I smiled. "Thank you, but with Stephanie and Lucky here, I feel safe. I do appreciate your concern. You and Stevie are invited for dinner tonight."

It took a lot of convincing to prevent him from coming over immediately, but I assured him there was no rush. The stranger was gone. We were all fine and, after his encounter with Lucky, I doubted that the man would be foolish enough to come back. Nevertheless, I made sure all of the doors were locked and the security alarm was engaged.

We chatted a bit longer, but then I reminded him about my need for coffee and the fact that I still had to get dressed.

I hung up and turned to Stephanie who was sitting on the floor with Lucky.

"Not a great introduction to my new neighborhood. I hope you won't be afraid to come back and visit me again."

She smiled. "Mom, I live in downtown Chicago. You have to develop a pretty tough skin to live there. Besides, I pity the fool who tries to rob you." She gave Aggie a scratch as the little dog tried to sneak in between Stephanie and Lucky's love fest.

"I don't understand this. The neighborhood has always been so safe." I shook my head. "I haven't told Red, but I've even left my garage door open all night and even though there are still boxes from the move, no one bothered anything."

She laughed. "In Chicago, they would have stripped that garage like locusts." She reached into her pocket and pulled out a small object.

"What's that?"

"A taser." She smiled. "You're not the only one dating someone in law enforcement."

I shook my head. "I honestly don't understand what's going on. I love this neighborhood. I love being close to businesses and people and still having privacy." I paused. "I know it isn't as fancy as the subdivision where I was renting, but...it makes me happy."

"That's what's important." Stephanie stood up and gave me a hug. "Besides, at least you haven't found any dead bodies in this neighborhood." She smiled before adding. "Yet."

I was silent for several moments.

"I was just kidding, Mom."

"I'm sorry, dear. I was just thinking. You know, I don't believe in coincidences, but I haven't had any problems until Archibald Lowry was murdered two days ago. Since then, someone has tried to steal Rex and an intruder has gotten into my backyard." I shook my head. "I may not have discovered a dead body, but I think I'm going to need to find a killer if I want to have peace."

"Alright, Sherlock." She clapped. "Let's get this investigation underway."

Chapter 7

During my great house hunting expedition a few months ago, I learned that Monica Jill was fearless behind the wheel of a car. Whether climbing a mountain or navigating treacherous country roads, our intrepid realtor handled them all with style and finesse. Since we were both going to the dog show and she knew my fear of driving up mountains, she offered to pick me up. Being the coward that I am, I accepted. I knew she would be fine with Stephanie and Lucky coming along, but good manners demanded that I ask anyway. Southern hospitality forced her to have her husband wash her car, vacuum all of the dog hair, bake a quiche and pick up coffee for all of us before she picked us up. I truly loved the South.

Monica Jill was as perky as ever when she arrived, but she wasn't alone.

"This beautiful young lady is Addison Abbott." She glanced toward the back seat while she made a sharp turn and picked up speed to get onto the interstate.

I grabbed the door handle and made sure my seat belt was securely fastened. Once we were cruising along with the other cars, I released my grip on the door. "Hello, Addison."

She giggled. "Please, call me Addy."

Addison Abbott looked to be about thirteen years old. She had long dark hair, dark eyes and long legs. She bore a slight resemblance to Monica Jill.

"Are you related?" I asked.

Monica Jill glanced at me briefly before crossing four lanes of traffic. "No, but thanks for the compliment. She's absolutely gorgeous." She chuckled. "Actually, Addy is the daughter of one of my coworkers, but she loves dogs and her dad was showing houses all day, so I suggested she come with us."

I tried to smile as Monica Jill veered back across four lanes of traffic, barely missing a semi, to take our exit. After a few moments, I swallowed the lump in my throat. "I'm sure we can use the help."

Addy snuggled the poodles close to her face. "I love dogs. I've got a big dog. She's half boxer and half pit bull."

"My boyfriend has a pit bull mix too." I opened my eyes and glanced at Addy. "His name is Steve Austin. You're probably too young to remember a TV show called the *Six Million Dollar Man,* but—"

"I know that one. My dad likes to watch old shows."

I tried not to notice the dig about the *old shows*. She was very young and to her, the eighties were probably ancient times. However, a sideways glance at Stephanie showed her fighting back a laugh. Thankfully, Addy was oblivious to any type of social faux pas.

"My dog's name is Mika," she continued.

Stephanie smiled. "That's a pretty name."

Once we left the interstate, Monica Jill stopped channeling Mario Andretti and I was able to open my eyes, release my grip on the handle at the top of the door that Red called the *OH MY GOD* handle, and enjoy the remainder of the drive. I learned that Addie was a straight A student who ran track and loved dogs. She reminded me a lot of Stephanie at that age.

When we arrived at the site for the dog show, Monica Jill parked. We unloaded all of the humans and dogs and went to Dixie's RV for breakfast. B.J. was already there when we arrived.

B.J. yawned. "Pass the coffee and remind me again why I agreed to come to a dog show at this ungodly hour on a Sunday morning?"

"How do you like your coffee?" Dixie asked.

B.J. smiled. "I like my coffee the same way I like my men. Strong, dark and sweet."

Dixie smiled and handed her a cup, then slid the sugar container toward her.

A long time ago in a land far away…or two days ago, before Archibald Lowry was murdered and someone tried to steal Rex and an intruder entered my yard, the members of Dixie's Eastern Tennessee Dog Club training class had arranged to meet for breakfast in Dixie's RV for last minute instructions. We all agreed to participate in a demonstration event showcasing the importance of training your dogs. This would be the first time that we would be *showcasing* what we'd learned in class outside of the ETDC training class. However, in light of recent events, I decided to use this opportunity to solicit help.

"You agreed to do it to support a worthwhile cause," Monica Jill reminded B.J. in her perky voice.

Monica Jill was in full makeup, with perfectly straight hair which I knew was the result of over an hour with a flat iron each morning and she was wearing a designer sweat suit.

B.J. looked as though she had just rolled out of bed. She had no makeup, was wearing a pair of old sweat pants with holes, a t-shirt and baseball cap. If looks could kill, Monica Jill would have dropped dead.

"Oh my, get this woman some more coffee." Monica Jill laughed.

B.J. pointed a finger and said, "You are entirely too perky."

Stephanie giggled from the sofa. Addy sat cross-legged on the floor covered in dogs of all shapes and sizes. Two standard poodles, two toy poodles, a German shepherd, a golden, a Westie and Jac, the border collie mix vied for the opportunity to lick her face.

B.J. sipped her coffee and glanced around. "Granite counters, stainless steel appliances and leather furniture. This is the nicest RV I've ever seen."

Monica Jill nodded. "I agree. This is bigger than some houses I've been in."

Dixie smiled. "When I was competing, I travelled all over. I spent a lot of time on the road and many of the really nice hotels don't take dogs. I wanted something that felt like home." She smiled at her husband. "Beau gave me this for our wedding anniversary one year."

Dixie's RV was massive. It had three extensions that made it wide and spacious. I knew there was a queen-sized bed in the back and eight people could sleep in here if push came to shove. Even with seven adults and eight dogs, Dixie's RV still felt luxuriously spacious.

"At one point, I thought it would be nice to have a mobile pet hotel or daycare," Dixie said.

Monica Jill smiled. "My goodness gracious, that would be so nice. You could send the RV to pick up the dogs and take them to the dog park."

"I always thought it would be great to have a doggie daycare downtown. People who worked there could drop off their pets on their way to the office and pick them up afterward." Dixie sighed.

Monica Jill smacked the table top with her hand. "I know the perfect location. There's a vacant building downtown near the Choo Choo."

The Choo Choo was named after the song "Chattanooga Choo Choo," but was now a hotel and shopping area rather than a railway station.

"That hotel doesn't take dogs, but if there was a daycare close by, people could bring their dogs with them on vacation and board them right across the street." Monica Jill looked excited. "I'm going to look up the listing."

Dixie held up a hand. "Hold up. That was only a dream."

Monica Jill swiped her phone. "Well, sister, this might just be the time to dust off that dream."

Dr. Morgan quietly drank coffee and listened.

Beau stood near the front and smiled. "Maybe I should set up the pen outside for the dogs."

"NO!" we all shouted.

Dixie turned to her startled husband. "Given what happened yesterday, we're all a bit reluctant about leaving the dogs unattended."

"They won't be unattended." He glanced pointedly at Addison. "Addy and I are on dog detail." He winked and reached for leashes. "Plus, this time I'll be ready for anyone who tries any funny business." He lifted his jacket exposing the gun he wore at his waist.

Stephanie and Addison stood up and each took several leashes. Addison was the most eager. "Maybe I should take them for a run around the park to help them burn off some energy."

Monica Jill smiled. "That would be great. I need Jac to burn a whole lot of energy."

Stephanie stretched. "I can help too, Uncle Beau."

Addison, Beau, Stephanie and the eight dogs left. The room suddenly felt quiet and somewhat lonely.

Dixie must have noticed the look of panic on my face. She patted my shoulder. "Don't worry, Beau is an excellent shot."

"I'm not worried about that, but is he allowed to have a weapon?" I whispered.

"Honey, this is Tennessee. Everybody has a weapon." She laughed. "More importantly, he has a permit to carry."

I tried to relax. I knew Beau and Stephanie would be on high alert for any strangers. I also knew they would do whatever it took to see that Addison and the dogs were safe. I took a deep breath, held it for a few moments and then slowly released it.

"Now, I think you're all ready for the demonstration." Dixie looked at each of us and we nodded in response. "Just try to remember to have fun. This is only a demonstration. It's not a real trial so there's no reason to be nervous. Just do what you've done so well the last few months in training."

"Training? What training? I don't remember no training," B.J. joked.

I waited until the laughter died down. "After our demonstration, I think we need to start asking a few questions."

"It's about time." Monica Jill smacked her hand on the table, causing a small quake and spilling some of the coffee out of our cups. She hurried to the counter and picked up a stack of napkins to clean up.

"What you got in mind?" B.J. asked.

"I don't know if there are a lot of people here who knew Archibald Lowry personally, but I was hoping we could ask around." I looked at Dixie.

"I know more of the people here than any of you." She looked around and we all nodded agreement. "Today there's going to be a small dedication and ceremony in Archibald Lowry's honor." She pulled out her cell phone and started scrolling. "I reached out to Lowry's butler to see if some of the people who knew him wanted to come." She looked up. "We'll have a small lunch and a brief memorial. I bought some flowers and have a little token of appreciation for each one of them."

"Great." I was always amazed at Dixie's thoughtfulness.

"Who's coming?" B.J. sipped her coffee.

Dixie scrolled and then stopped. "His lawyer, a Mr. Eli Goldstein; his butler and security guard, a man named Ivan Bradington; his housekeeper, Mrs. Catherine Huntington; and his chauffeur, Paul Carpenter."

"My goodness, how many people worked for this man?" B.J. stopped drinking coffee to stare.

Dixie sighed. "No idea, but I know he also had a gamekeeper." She scrolled. "No name is listed but I'll find out. Oh, and there are Fergus and Mary Kilpatrick." She glanced up. "They are apparently distant cousins who had come from Scotland for a visit."

"How sad." Monica Jill shook her head. "They came all this way to visit their cousin only to have him brutally murdered."

We all agreed the situation was sad, but then quickly moved on.

"Now, how are we going to do this?" B.J. asked.

Everyone turned and looked at me.

I hadn't thought through all of the details, so I reverted to the technique that had worked well for us in the past. "Well, I thought maybe we could divide and conquer."

"Good idea." Dixie nodded. "We can make sure that Stephanie sits next to the lawyer." She glanced around. "She can ask him questions and it might seem more natural coming from one lawyer to another."

We all nodded.

"Why don't I tackle the chauffeur?" B.J. asked.

We nodded again.

"Maybe, I can sell him an insurance policy if nothing else."

Monica Jill raised her hand. "I'd like to take Mary and Fergus Kilpatrick." She looked around. "Unless you or Dixie would rather?"

We shook our heads.

I turned to Dixie. "I know you're going to be really busy with the trial, but I was hoping you could ask around, maybe start with the housekeeper and see if she has any useful information."

She nodded.

"The housekeeper and any of the poodle lovers out there." I looked at her. "I mean, the man was a poodle fanatic, surely someone in the poodle community knows something that might be useful."

"Great." A thought formed in the back of my mind, and I turned to Dr. Morgan. "Dixie said Archibald Lowry became the Scottish Laird and had poodles and sheep and a host of other animals."

Dr. Morgan narrowed his gaze and raised an eyebrow, not liking the direction my thoughts were going.

"Do you think you could find out who the gamekeeper was and have a talk with him?"

"I'm a doctor, not a veterinarian."

"Uh huh, hold on there, big boy." B.J. gave the doctor a hard stare. "I'm an insurance agent, not a chauffeur, but I'm helping."

"And Dixie isn't a housekeeper, but she's going to talk to his housekeeper," Monica Jill added.

He held up both hands. "I'm sorry. I didn't mean any offense." He sighed. "I'll do it, but I don't see how it can help. I mean even if he is willing to talk to me, what kind of information will he be able to provide that could possibly help us find out who killed Archibald Lowry."

"Well, whoever killed Archibald Lowry had to be someone who knew him." I paused and glanced around. "From what I've heard, his circle of friends is pretty small, so it would need to be someone close to him."

Everyone nodded.

"Besides, I can't believe it's a coincidence that the day after Archibald Lowry was killed someone tries to steal his dog and then someone breaks into my yard."

"You think all of this is connected?" Dixie asked.

I shrugged. "It has to be. Those are just too many coincidences for me."

She nodded. "You're right. The poodle community is a small, tight-knit community. Recluse or not, someone out there has to know something helpful."

"What are you going to do?" Dixie asked me.

"I'm going to see what I can get out of the butler."

"Plus, I think the biggest question I want answered is what was he protecting Archibald Lowry from? People don't hire bodyguards unless they feel threatened." I glanced around. "And I want to know who was threatening him."

Chapter 8

The obedience demonstrations went surprisingly well, despite a few glitches. Dr. Morgan accidentally tripped on his German shepherd's foot while demonstrating how to heel and fell flat on his backside, which garnered a great deal of laughter once the crowd realized he was uninjured.

Dixie wasn't just the judge during our demonstration. She held a microphone and provided color commentary, which kept the audience engaged even during our mistakes.

My only error came when I had a moment of absentmindedness and loosened the slack on Aggie's leash. Overcome with joy, she took off running, pulling the leash from my hands. She got what we all called the zoomies. She took several laps around the ring, her mouth open and tongue hanging out with a look of pure glee on her little face. She ran at top speed in circles, with me frantically chasing her. Just when I got close and bent down to get her leash, she would make a sharp turn and head in a different direction, her leash trailing behind.

Dixie chuckled for a few moments and then sent one of her poodles into the ring, knowing Aggie wouldn't be able to resist playing with her friends. When Chyna got close to Aggie, Dixie gave her a command to lay down, which the well-behaved standard poodle obeyed immediately. Aggie dropped into her play bow, with front paws down and butt in the air long enough for me to get a foot on her leash. I quickly scooped Aggie up and carried her away.

I didn't need a mirror to know that my face was red. I looked for a giant hole to slink into but forced myself to stand by and listen to the laughter from the crowd.

Dixie used the opportunity to explain that Aggie was a young poodle with lots of energy, but that one day she would be as well-behaved as her adopted cousins, Chyna and Leia, with a little more guidance and direction. Dixie finished the event by demonstrating some of the more advanced obedience skills that her dogs knew.

The demonstration took less than thirty minutes, but it felt like hours. Monica Jill and B.J. hugged me when it was over which made me feel worse than if they had just ignored me. Dr. Morgan gave me a sympathetic nod, before he and Max headed out in the general direction of the main house. Stephanie walked over, cuddling Rex. "You look like you could use a hug." Instead of hugging me, she handed over Rex and took Aggie's leash from my hands.

Rex cuddled me for a few seconds and then proceeded to give my face a thorough tongue washing which made me smile.

"It wasn't as bad as you think," Dixie said as she came up beside me.

"Yeah, right."

"Trust me, after showing dogs for well over twenty years, I have stories that would make your experience feel like a walk in the park."

I stared at her. "Try me."

"During my first conformation show, I showed a beautiful white standard poodle, Candy. She was the most gorgeous dog I'd ever seen and I knew she would win. She just had to. She was incredible." She paused for a moment as she reminisced about the dog. Then she shook her head and continued. "My mentor told me to make sure I always took my dogs out to potty at least twice before a show. Well, I was rushing, and she'd peed and pooped less than thirty minutes earlier, so I figured it was safe to skip the second potty run." She tilted her head and gave me a hard stare. "That was a mistake. I got in the ring and all was going well. The judge examined her and she showed beautifully. She was groomed to perfection and I knew it. Then he sent us around the ring so he could check the gait." She shook her head and sighed. "We started trotting around the ring and that's when that stinker stopped right there and pooped. I wasn't paying attention and kept going until I felt the pull on the leash. When I turned to look to see what the holdup was, I was mortified. Unfortunately, I wasn't watching where I was going, and tripped and fell." She looked at me.

"Oh no. You didn't fall into—"

She nodded. "Face first."

"Oh My God, Dixie."

"To make matters worse, I was wearing a white suit."

The mental image of my beautiful, well dressed friend falling into dog poop shouldn't have incited laughter, but I couldn't help it. "Oh, Dixie. I'm sorry." I laughed. "What did you do?"

"I got up, wiped the poop off as best as I could, and kept going." She shook her head. "You know what the really remarkable thing was?" She stared at me.

I shook my head.

"We won our first major and Best in Show."

I laughed. "Dixie, I can't imagine you wearing a poop covered suit all day."

"Well, I couldn't wear the suit all day. I smelled horrible." She shook her head. "I ended up borrowing a suit from a friend."

I bowed. "You win. That is a lot worse."

She nodded. "After that show I told Beau we needed an RV with a shower." She shuddered at the memory. "I keep at least three suits and several pairs of shoes in the RV at all times in case of emergency." She smiled. "If there's one thing you learn about showing dogs, you better leave your pride at home."

I gave my friend a warm hug. "Thank you. I honestly, didn't think anyone could pull me out of the dumps, but you did."

She squeezed me. "Sadly, that's not the most embarrassing thing that's ever happened."

I pulled away and stared. "You have got to be kidding."

"Not even close."

"I can't wait to hear what could be worse than falling in dog poop."

"Nope." She shook her head. "I'm saving those stories for later, when you and Aggie are actually competing for real and not just doing a demonstration." She laughed.

B.J. tapped me on the shoulder. "I think I see my mark."

I followed her glance which was directed toward a long black limousine that had pulled into the grounds. A short man dressed in an all-black chauffeur's uniform, complete with cap, hurried to open the rear door. A couple climbed out and glanced around.

B.J. handed Stephanie her West Highland Terrier's leash and hurried to the limo.

"I think I just saw mine, too." Monica Jill smiled big, handed Stephanie Jac's leash, and hurried over to the couple.

Stephanie deftly juggled leashes for Lucky, Snoball and Jac. After adjusting the dogs, she looked up and gasped.

I turned to see what had caught her attention. That's when I looked up into the deepest blue eyes I'd ever seen. Standing a few feet away stood six feet and two hundred pounds of pure muscle wrapped in dark jeans and a crisp white shirt which contrasted well with his tanned arms. He had dark, wavy hair and a neatly trimmed moustache and beard.

He smiled at Dixie. "Excuse me, are you Scarlet Jefferson?"

We all stared for several seconds before Dixie collected herself.

"Call me Dixie." She extended her hand.

He shook her hand. "I'm Eli Goldstein, Archibald Lowry's lawyer."

Eli Goldstein waited for an awkward few seconds.

I gave Dixie a gentle push which worked to jar her out of her stupor. "Oh, pardon my manners. This is my friend, Lilly Ann Echosby."

I shook.

She turned to Stephanie. "And this is Lilly's daughter, Stephanie."

The air crackled with static electricity.

Stephanie and the bronzed Adonis shook hands and gazed into each other's eyes.

There's no telling how long we would have stayed there staring if Lucky, Snoball, Jac, and Aggie hadn't broken the spell.

For whatever reason, the golden lunged forward and the other dogs managed to get around Stephanie's legs. She would have fallen forward if Eli hadn't reached out to grab her and broken her fall.

Righted, but still wrapped up in the dog leashes, Stephanie worked to extricate herself. Finally, free, she looked down at Lucky who was still lunging at the handsome stranger.

"I don't know what's gotten into him. He's usually so friendly."

Eli smiled and flashed the whitest, most perfectly straight teeth I've seen in quite some time. "It's just a bit of male possessiveness. He doesn't like another male admiring his beautiful owner."

Stephanie blushed and looked around for help. "Where's Addison?"

Just at that moment we saw Addy coming toward us eating a donut. When she got to us, the dogs got a whiff of the sugar and immediately started pawing at the teen for a bite of the donut.

Dixie took Lucky's leash. "Why don't you let us take Lucky and the other dogs back to the RV with the rest of the pack."

Eli's eyes widened. "Rest? You mean there's more?"

We left Stephanie to explain as Dixie and I walked back to the RV. Beau was inside with Chyna and Leia. They were lying on the sofa watching a football game. When we entered, he sat up. "Welcome to the Jefferson travelling pet emporium."

We chuckled and removed all of the dogs' leashes and allowed them to mix, mingle and sniff each other's butts as though they were total strangers. We waited a few minutes to ensure all was under control.

Donut consumed, Addison sat on the floor and played with the dogs. Dixie and I stood near the window, looking out at Stephanie and Eli as they stood together and talked. From our viewpoint, the two looked to be enjoying themselves and made a great looking pair.

"What do you think about that gorgeous hunk?" Dixie inclined her head toward the pair.

Before I could respond, Beau stood up, puffed out his chest and rubbed his stomach. "Thank you, I've been working out. Glad you noticed."

We laughed.

After I regained my composure, I took another glance at Stephanie. "Well, I don't know. He seems nice and he's definitely handsome, but…I don't know. I really like Joe. He's such a good guy and—"

Dixie sighed. "Oh, thank goodness. I feel the same way."

We glanced at each other and chuckled.

"He's great to look at, but…well, he's more eye candy than the settle down, clean the bathroom and let's weather the storms of life together kind of man." She glanced lovingly at Beau who had returned to the sofa with Aggie, Rex and Snoball lying on his chest. Chyna, Lucky and Leia were sprawled out on their sides on the floor next to him. Periodically, Beau would toss a red rubber ball to the back of the RV and Jac would leap into the air and chase it. Eventually, he would return the ball and Beau would repeat.

"That's exactly what I mean." I smiled as we quietly headed to the door and walked down the steps.

Eli and Stephanie turned toward us as we approached.

"Mr. Goldstein, I'm so glad you were able to make it today," Dixie said.

"Please, call me Eli. Mr. Goldstein is my father." He flashed a smile that caused each of us to giggle. "I'm glad to be here, although I wish it was for a more pleasant occasion."

We wiped the smiles off our faces and nodded, now that we were brought back to the seriousness of Mr. Archibald Lowry's death.

I awkwardly mumbled condolences, but Dixie truly shone when it came to expressing grief and knowing the appropriate thing to say in all situations. She placed one hand over her heart and another on Eli's arm. "Please accept all of our condolences. We didn't know Archibald very well, but it must be horrible for those of you who did know him. Were you very close?"

Eli nodded. "Well I wouldn't say that Archibald Lowry allowed himself to get *close* to anyone, but I've worked for him for a number of years."

"Are you in private practice?" Stephanie asked.

Eli nodded. "Yes, guilty as charged." He chuckled. "I'm afraid a small practice isn't nearly as exciting as working for a big firm in a city like Chicago." He gazed at Stephanie with awe and a healthy dose of respect.

She shrugged. "I don't know about exciting, but it's definitely interesting."

He gazed at Stephanie. "Maybe, we could compare notes over dinner." When she hesitated, he hurriedly added, "Unless there is a Mr. Echosby or someone other than the golden retriever I need to contend with." He reached down and held her left hand. "It's just I didn't notice a wedding ring, so…" He shrugged.

Stephanie gazed into his eyes for several seconds. She reached out a hand and picked two strands of red hair from his shoulder.

Eli took the hairs and dropped them, then dusted off his pants. "I must be covered in dog hair after the greeting I got today."

Stephanie smiled. "Dog hair comes with the territory." She shrugged. "As to dinner…sure, why not?"

He turned up the smile wattage and beamed. "Great." He tucked her arm in his and they ambled over to the tent which was set up for lunch.

Dixie and I walked slowly behind the couple, but were halted by a commotion. We turned to see what was happening.

Dr. Morgan and Max were marching toward the tent, followed by a petite Asian woman with a long ponytail wearing forest green rubber chest waders that were held up by suspenders that went over each shoulder. She was accompanied by a medium-sized dog with unusual coloring.

Dixie gasped. "What a beautiful border collie."

"It is beautiful, but I thought border collies were black and white, like Jac," I said.

"Black and white is very common but they can come in a variety of colors. Red, black, sable, saddleback sable, white and black, liver and white, blue tricolor, red merle…there's a ton of different colors." She inclined her head toward the regal beast that was circling behind the two humans. "That's a red merle."

"What's merle?"

"Merle is created when a gene in one of the parents is incomplete. It's hereditary and it takes a dominant gene and dilutes it creating a splotchy, swirl pattern."

The group got closer and I got a better look at the dog who had a very intense stare. "Border Collies give me the creeps. The way they stare. Does that dog have blue eyes?"

"She does have blue eyes. Border collies can have blue or brown eyes. Just like in humans, brown is more common and the stare is normal. They are remarkably intelligent dogs, bred in Scotland as working and herding dogs. They're sometimes called Scottish sheep dogs."

"Not surprising. Archibald Lowry loved all things Scottish."

She smiled. "She's watching, waiting for something to move so she can herd it." She paused. "They're amazing working dogs and great with obedience, agility and other performance events. In fact, they are so dominant in agility, some clubs are hosting Border Collie only trials. This breed is definitely not one for lounging on the sofa watching television. These dogs need a job, or they can get into trouble."

When the doctor got close enough to us, we could see his face was red and his heavy breathing had nothing to do with the walk he'd just taken. He was angry.

He marched up to where Dixie and I were standing, turned to the woman and said, "For the last time, I'm not a veterinarian."

Undeterred, the woman pulled herself up to her full height, which appeared to be about five feet tall and pointed a finger in his face. "You're a medical doctor and Maisie needs medical attention. The least you can do is *try* and help."

The border collie sat by her owner's side, staring. Surprisingly, Max, who was normally very active, sat by his owner's side and stared at the border collie.

Dr. Morgan turned to us and held out his hands. "Can you please tell this…woman, that I am a medical doctor and do not work on cows."

Dixie's lips twitched, but she quickly collected herself and turned to the woman. "What's wrong with Maisie?"

The woman scowled at Dr. Morgan. "She's giving birth, but something's wrong. Our usual vet is in the middle of emergency surgery. So, when this guy," she turned to give Dr. Morgan another scowl, "came wandering by, I thought he would help." She spat. "Instead, he just said, I'm not a vet," she said in a beautiful clipped British accent and then folded her arms across her chest.

Dixie turned to Dr. Morgan. She softened her face and her eyes pleaded. "Couldn't you just—"

"No. I couldn't just. I don't know the first thing about birthing cows."

Dixie glanced at me and the twinkle in her eyes told me she had the exact same quote going through her head that went through mine. Eventually, we were unable to contain ourselves and burst out laughing.

Dr. Morgan stared from me to Dixie as though we'd suddenly lost our minds. "What on earth is so funny?"

Dixie recovered first. She turned up her southern accent and said in her best Butterfly McQueen, *Gone with the Wind* accent, "I don't know nothing' 'bout birthing babies."

Dixie and I started laughing again.

Dr. Morgan didn't see the humor, although I thought I detected a slight quiver at the lips of our Asian friend.

When we collected ourselves, Dixie turned to face the woman. "My name is Dixie Jefferson. You must be Mr. Lowry's gamekeeper."

The woman uncrossed her arms and nodded. "Yes. My name's Mai, Mai Nguyen."

They shook hands.

"I love your accent. Where—"

Mai straightened up to her full height, five-feet-nothing, and tilted her head. She then bowed her head in a subservient fashion and spoke in broken English. "Ah, you expect me talk like Vietnamese servant." She bowed several times but then stood up, put a hand on her hip and stared. "Sorry, they didn't teach me to speak that way at Cambridge."

Dixie held up her hands in surrender. "I didn't mean any offense. I just love your accent. I'm very sorry. I wasn't trying to insult you in any way."

Mai nodded. "I'm sorry too. I guess, I shouldn't have assumed you were as bigoted and close minded as some of the people I've met since I've come here." She held out her hand. "Please forgive my rude behavior."

Dixie shook. "Only if you will forgive mine." All was forgiven. Then she inclined her head toward the border collie. "And who's your friend?"

Mai gave a genuine smile. "This is Skye."

"May I?" Dixie asked.

Mai nodded.

"That's a good Scottish name." Dixie squatted down and permitted Skye to sniff her. When she was satisfied, Dixie ran her hands down the dog's coat and whispered soothing words of nonsense to her. When she'd finished, she gave the dog a pat.

Dixie stood up and I nudged her.

"I'm sorry, this is my friend, Lilly Ann Echosby."

I extended my hand to Mai and we shook.

Dixie glanced quickly at her watch and then took Dr. Morgan by the arm and Mai by the other and started slowly walking back in the direction they'd just come. "Now, I'm sure we can figure out a solution to this problem if we just put our heads together."

Skye, Max and I followed as Dixie guided Dr. Morgan and Mai back through the woods, all the time talking. She alternated between asking questions and making statements designed to stroke egos and de-escalate the situation. She chatted nonstop about everything from *Mai is a beautiful name. What's the origin?* to *Dr. Morgan is so intelligent, I just know he'll be able to help us come up with a solution."*

It didn't take long before we came out of the woods to a fenced field with cows.

We climbed over the fence and walked toward a large cow that was lying on its side under an oak tree.

I assumed this had to be Maisie. Based on the amount of noise she was making, she wasn't happy. She had a steady drip of mucus and what appeared to be a hoof coming out of her rear.

Mai went to the animal and stroked her head, whispering calming words. Skye paced back and forth, anxiously awaiting someone to move.

I was a city girl and wasn't very fond of farm animals, but even I felt compassion at the sounds coming from that poor animal as she struggled to give birth. I turned to Dr. Morgan. "She sounds miserable. Surely, there's something you can do to help her?"

Dr. Morgan stared at each of us and then handed me Max's leash. He pulled out his cell phone and walked a short distance away as he pressed the buttons.

If I hadn't been holding Max, I might have been concerned that he meant to leave, but when he finished, he marched back over and rolled up his sleeves. "Okay, I'm going to need a towel and some rope."

Mai nodded and ran toward a barn followed by Skye.

Dixie knelt down and took her place, stroking Maisie and whispering sweet nothings into her ear.

Dr. Morgan positioned himself at the business end of the beast and said, "Dixie Jefferson you owe me big time for this." He shoved his arm into the cow's rear and reached inside. "The calf is backward. I need to turn it."

He gave a tug. Maisie mooed and I struggled to keep from puking.

Mai ran back from the barn carrying rope and several towels. She placed everything at Dr. Morgan's feet.

Dr. Morgan was still shoulder deep inside the cow's rear, but that didn't stop him from giving orders. "The calf is twisted. The head needs to come out first. I'm going to try and turn it." He finagled something that caused Maisie to moan even more loudly.

Dr. Morgan made another twist and then gave a pull. He slowly removed his arm. Like the creature coming out of Sigourney Weaver's stomach in the movie, *Aliens*, something pulsed and twisted and eventually popped out of the cow's rear. Dr. Morgan tied one end of the rope to the hoof and tugged.

Maisie pushed and eventually a head appeared, covered in a film of mucus. Maisie gave one more big groan and then pushed the calf out onto the ground.

Dr. Morgan removed the rope from the calf's foot and pulled some of the film away from the head.

I held my breath and waited while Dr. Morgan and Mai worked. It was only when I saw the calf move that I released the breath I'd been holding.

Mai was so excited she reached up and gave a hoop and then threw herself in Dr. Morgan's arms and hugged him. The doctor seemed dazed, but managed a one-armed hug. When she released him, he used one of the towels to clean himself up.

We stood by and watched as Maisie licked away the remaining mucus and the calf struggled to adapt to its new environment.

Dixie squatted down and had a few words with Mai and then she stood up and smiled at Dr. Morgan. "I knew you could do it."

"I need a shower," he mumbled.

Dixie stood up. "Let's go back to the RV. You can get a shower and I'm sure Beau has some extra clothes you can wear."

Chapter 9

Dr. Morgan showered and changed but wasn't in the mood for lunch. Instead, he announced that he wanted to go and check on his patient. The color I saw rising up his neck made me suspect the calf wasn't the only thing he wanted to check on.

Addison leapt up. "Can I come see the calf?"

Dr. Morgan nodded. He, Max, Addison, Lucky and Jac headed back through the woods. Before they left, Dixie called to Dr. Morgan. "I wonder if you could do a slight favor for me?"

The doctor narrowed his eyes. "What kind of favor? I am not delivering any more farm animals."

Dixie chuckled. "Nothing like that." She smiled. "It's just that Mai agreed to help me out on Tuesday. I've got a demonstration at a middle school and she agreed to let me borrow a few sheep and Skye to do a herding demonstration."

Addison clapped. "That's going to be at my school. Can I help with the demonstration?"

Dixie nodded. "Of course, dear." She turned to Dr. Morgan. "It's just that in all of the excitement, I forgot to get Mai's telephone number. I was hoping you could get that for me." She paused and then quickly added, "So, I can make sure she has all of the information."

Dr. Morgan's neck got red, but he nodded.

"Thank you so much. I'm sure I can find someone at the school to help with loading and unloading the sheep." She looked at the coroner expectantly and was rewarded.

"I might be able to help with that, too."

She clapped her hands. "That would be wonderful. Maybe you could work out the details with Mai and just let me know what you two figure out."

He nodded and then headed for the woods with Addison and the dogs.

Dixie changed from her grass-stained jeans into a fresh outfit and I looked around the lunch tent.

B.J., Monica Jill and Stephanie were sitting at a large table with all of the people from Archibald Lowry's household. Eli was seated in between Stephanie and B.J. and looked uncomfortable, but that probably had more to do with the goo-goo eyes he was getting from B.J. than any vibes he might have picked up from Stephanie.

I sat down at the table in the seat next to Stephanie that she had saved for me while Dixie stood up at the front. She welcomed all of the visitors and thanked everyone for coming. She spent several minutes thanking Archibald Lowry for being such a great supporter and allowing the East Tennessee Poodle Rescue to have their fundraiser on his property.

Everyone applauded politely.

After a few moments, Dixie continued.

"As everyone must be aware by now, Archibald Lowry was brutally murdered a few days ago."

There was a loud flurry of whispers.

"However, thanks to his wonderful staff, we were able to still hold our event here today."

More applause.

"I'd like to take just a moment to publicly thank Mr. Eli Goldstein, Archibald Lowry's lawyer."

Eli Goldstein surprised me by blushing at the recognition. The handsome lawyer didn't strike me as someone who would shun attention, but maybe I misjudged the man simply because he was handsome. He gave a reluctant wave and gulped water from the bottle at his place setting.

Dixie called off the other names and each person rose in turn. "Mrs. Catherine Huntington, who I understand was Archibald Lowry's housekeeper for over twenty years." The housekeeper stood. She seemed nervous and clutched a cross around her neck. She inclined her head in a brief bow and sat. "Paul Carpenter, Archibald Lowry's chauffeur."

He rose and waved.

Dixie continued. "Ivan Bradington, butler."

Bradington was the only person who wasn't seated, preferring instead to stand in true butler-like manner near the side of the tent. When his name was called, he took one step forward and gave a slight bow before stepping backward.

"Last, but not least, I want to introduce Archibald Lowry's cousins who travelled all the way from Scotland to visit with him, Mary and Fergus Kilpatrick."

Monica Jill applauded enthusiastically as the two stood up and waved at the crowd.

When the applause died down, Dixie asked everyone to close their eyes, bow their heads and observe a few moments of silence in honor of Archibald Lowry. After a few moments, Dixie thanked everyone for their hard work. "Now, if everyone would take a glass of the champagne which is sitting in front of their seats, let's raise a glass to Archibald Lowry."

Everyone picked up their glass of amber liquid. The glasses were plastic flutes, but all things considered, it was a nice gesture.

"To Archibald Lowry."

We lifted our glasses. "Archibald Lowry."

I noticed Lowry's housekeeper didn't drink, but merely held her glass.

"Now, please enjoy your lunch." Dixie sat down at the seat next to me at the head table. She leaned over and whispered, "Normally, we're lucky if we get soggy sub sandwiches and bags of stale chips, but Archibald Lowry insisted on traditional Scottish fare and had his housekeeper arrange for the meal."

The meal was three courses which included a small salad with a dollop of salad dressing, and a bread and butter pudding.

The chauffeur took one look at his plate, scrunched his nose, pushed his plate away, then reached over and got the bottle of champagne on the table and topped his glass. He gulped it down, refilled his glass and repeated.

I decided to chalk his bad behavior up to grief and returned my attention to my plate. I turned to Dixie and whispered, "Is this what I think it is?"

She nodded and forced a smile. "Traditional Scottish cuisine."

"Oh, yum."

Dixie and I exchanged glances but held our tongues. Surprisingly, Mary Kilpatrick had the same puzzled look that I saw on B.J.'s face.

The housekeeper, Mrs. Catherine Huntington, was seated directly across from me. I looked up and smiled. I felt sure she saw me, but she didn't return my smile. Instead, I saw a look of fear flash across her face. Her hand shook and she clasped the crucifix and medallion she wore around her neck. It seemed to have a steadying effect on her. The fear I'd seen moments before quickly vanished. She released the cross and medal, reached across and pointed out each item. "haggis, black pudding, turnips and potatoes."

I nodded. I knew what haggis was and felt confident that B.J. and Monica Jill wouldn't appreciate the cuisine.

B.J. frowned. "What's haggis?"

Mary Kilpatrick took a sip of water and smiled like someone from a foreign country who doesn't understand the language. After a few moments, she looked up and said, "I'm afraid I don't cook much."

Mrs. Huntington grunted. "It's the lamb pluck." She must have noticed the puzzled look on B.J.'s face because she elaborated. "The innards, heart, kidneys and lungs mixed with onions, spices, oatmeal and cooked in the intestines."

I wasn't sure what type of reaction I expected from B.J., but I wasn't anticipating delight.

She turned to Mary. "Oh, sort of like chitlins?"

Now, it was Mary's turn to look confused. "Chitlins? I don't know what that is?"

Monica Jill smiled. "It's chit-ter-lings," she enunciated. "Pork intestines."

Mary Kilpatrick looked as though she wanted to puke but forced a smile instead.

B.J. turned to Monica Jill. "What do you know about chitlins?"

Monica Jill scowled. "I know what they are. I see them in tubs at the grocery store."

"Ever had any?"

"No," Monica Jill said. "I haven't, but I've smelled them and that was enough for me."

B.J. prodded the round mound on her plate with her fork. "Now, what's *black pudding?* Is it some kind of dessert?"

Mary shrugged and turned to Mrs. Huntington. "Perhaps, we should consult the expert."

Catherine Huntington grunted. "It's a sausage made with pork jowls and blood."

I watched as B.J. shrugged and then took a small bite. "I'm not a big fan, but I guess it's an acquired taste." She took another bite. "Maybe it'll grow on me."

I've never been so proud of B.J. in my entire life. I pride myself on being open-minded, but I'd tried haggis and black pudding when Dixie and I had traveled through England and Scotland in college and I wasn't a fan.

I leaned close to Dixie and whispered, "Isn't real haggis banned in the U.S.?"

She nodded. "The Department of Agriculture doesn't allow it to be imported because of the lungs." She inclined her head toward the back of the tent where I saw the caterer. "Archibald was determined to have real haggis, but when I dug my heels in on importing illegal meat products, he compromised." She puffed her chest out in an imitation of Archibald

Lowry. "If I can't import the haggis, then I'll import the chef and have it made properly." She glanced around to make sure no one overheard her.

"That must have cost a small fortune and taken an incredibly long time."

She shrugged. "I suppose that's one of the perks of having more money than you know what to do with." She shook her head. "I assured him we could survive with only the black pudding and skip the haggis, but he was one determined man."

Paul Carpenter, the chauffeur, must have been listening because he leaned close to us. "Determined? Determined you call it. Archibald Lowry was stubborn, that's what I call it." He looked around. "Always, everything has to be done his way."

Dixie and I glanced around, but none of the other guests were offended by the chauffeur's statements.

"I suppose that's how he acquired his wealth…through determination or stubbornness." I mashed the haggis and black pudding with my fork and moved it around on the plate in an attempt to make it look as though I'd eaten at least some of it.

Paul Carpenter snorted. "Determination? You think determination is what made Archibald Lowry rich?" He chuckled and took another drink.

Eli Goldstein made eye contact with the chauffeur. "It's rude to speak ill of the dead."

Carpenter sneered. "Me? You call me rude? I'm an honest man. I speak the same things now that I said when he was alive. I don't pretend." He thumped his chest. "I don't claim to be something I'm not. I don't argue with someone and once he's dead, pretend that we didn't disagree." He drained his glass then pushed his chair back, stood and walked over to Mrs. Huntington. He reached down and took her glass. "You going to drink this?" He smiled big.

Mrs. Huntington shook her head, closed her eyes and grasped her comfort crucifix.

The chauffeur laughed and then drank Mrs. Huntington's champagne and replaced the glass on the table. He then walked over to a nearby table where there was another bottle of champagne. Grabbing the bottle, he brought it back to our table, and flopped down in his seat. This time he decided to forego using the glass and simply drank directly from the bottle.

Eli Goldstein leaned forward and attempted to take the bottle away, which was a big mistake.

Paul Carpenter wasn't ready to relinquish his bottle. He pushed Eli who fell backward to the ground.

Everyone in the tent stopped eating to watch the commotion at the head table.

The butler quickly hurried over to Paul Carpenter and whispered something into his ear. With one hand Ivan Bradington pinched a nerve in the chauffeur's neck, which caused the man to twitch. He then twisted his arm behind his back and hoisted him to his feet.

Carpenter grimaced while Bradington smiled. "Just a bit too much bubbly. Please excuse us." He turned and escorted the chauffeur out of the back of the tent.

After a few seconds, the crowd noise returned as the stunned group conferred about what had just happened.

I stared at Dixie. "What just happened?"

She shrugged.

Catherine Huntington's face seemed frozen with fear. Her gaze went from Eli Goldstein to Fergus Kilpatrick and then to the empty seat vacated by the chauffeur. She released her hold on the crucifix she wore around her neck long enough to cross herself, but then returned her hold.

Eli Goldstein regained his seat amidst sympathetic inquiries from Stephanie, B.J. and Monica Jill.

The lawyer looked flushed under his tan, but reassured everyone that the only thing injured was his pride.

"Come on." Dixie excused herself and headed out the back of the tent.

Thankful for any excuse to avoid eating anything further, I followed suit. As I left the tent, I got a glimpse of someone hurrying around the back of the tent. I stopped and tried to remember where I'd seen that face before.

"What's wrong?" Dixie asked.

I shrugged and shook my head as she grabbed me by the arm and pulled me along with her.

"Come on."

I quickly forgot the blur and hurried after my friend.

Outside, we saw the butler engaged in what appeared to be an animated and heated conversation with the chauffeur. The exchange was brief and after a few moments, the chauffeur slunk away.

Dixie approached the butler and I followed. "Anything we can help with?"

"No." The butler's eyes flashed briefly, but the look was instantly replaced with the blank expression he'd worn earlier. "I'm sorry you had to witness that. I assure you that Mr. Carpenter will be dealt with." He bowed and marched away.

Dixie and I stared after the butler for a few moments.

"What do you suppose was behind all of that?"

Dixie shook her head. "I have no idea, but I doubt it had anything to do with haggis."

Chapter 10

After lunch, Dixie, B.J., Stephanie, and I waited in Dixie's RV. Monica Jill wanted to see the new calf and volunteered to go and bring Dr. Morgan back.

Aggie was curled up on my shoulder, like a parrot, while Rex snuggled in my lap. I stared down at the cute bundle of fur and realized I was sinking deeper and deeper into the abyss. If Archibald Lowry's will left this little dog to someone else, my heart will have a poodle-sized hole. These thoughts prompted me to turn to Stephanie. "Did Mr. Lowry's attorney mention anything about his will?"

Stephanie looked at me with compassion. "Eli doesn't think he made arrangements for the dog," she paused, "which seems really weird." She looked sad. "Eli thought the cousins, Mary and Fergus Kilpatrick, might want him."

I hugged Rex close. "Maybe they'd let me buy him?"

Dixie patted my arm. "Honestly, I can't believe Archibald didn't make arrangements for his dog."

B.J. sat on a swivel chair and ate chips and tuna fish sandwiches, which Dixie had thoughtfully brought in case we weren't fans of the Scottish cuisine. "I read somewhere it's hard to get dogs into the United Kingdom. Don't they require pets to be quarantined for six months?"

Dixie shook her head. "That was true years ago, but they've relaxed their laws considerably and it's a lot easier to travel with dogs, cats, even ferrets."

"Six months? That's a long time to be away from your pet." I looked down at Rex and gave Aggie an extra cuddle. I couldn't imagine leaving my dog for half of the year.

"The United Kingdom had a really harsh ban in place for years to prevent rabies. But for the last two decades, they have made it a lot easier to bring animals into the country."

"Easier?" Beau snorted. "Isn't there a three-week wait period?"

Dixie nodded. "Three weeks from the time your dog is vaccinated, plus you have to have blood work done and..." She shook her head. "I used to know all of the rules when I was actively showing my dogs. Crufts is the British equivalent to the Westminster Dog Show. Preparing Leia and Chyna for that was a full-time job." She sighed. "They have something called the PETS Scheme. There's a list of approved countries that are allowed to bring pets into and out of the country. In addition to the vaccinations and blood tests, your dog will need to have your vet complete a certificate and then your dog has to be treated for tape worm."

"They even have rules about the ink the vet can use," Beau added.

"You're joking?" B.J. asked.

"Sadly, he isn't." Dixie shook her head. "They take this very seriously and if your pet's documentation isn't completed properly, that's it."

I looked down at Rex. "I guess that means I've got at least three weeks before the Kilpatricks will be able to take him."

Stephanie reached across and gave my hand a squeeze. "We'll figure something out before then."

There was a knock on the door of the RV and Addison, Monica Jill, Dr. Morgan, Max, Lucky and Jac entered.

"My God, that calf is just the cutest thing." Monica Jill washed her hands in the sink and then sat down at the table next to B.J. and helped herself to a sandwich and chips. "It has the biggest brown eyes and longest eyelashes I've ever seen."

"Hmm." B.J. rolled her own eyes and took a swig of her coke.

"What?" Monica Jill looked at her.

"How many calf's eyelashes have you seen?" She stared at her friend.

Monica Jill hesitated a moment and then chuckled. "Okay, well maybe that's the first calf I've ever seen up close and personal, but it was still cute."

We laughed.

Dr. Morgan washed his hands and then joined us at the large table. "It's certainly the first calf I've ever seen up close and personal."

"You and Maisie were definitely close." Dixie chuckled. "Tell the girls about your first calf delivery."

Dr. Morgan blushed, but told about the calf being twisted and how he had to turn it so it could be delivered.

B.J. squirmed. "You mean you had to put your arm all the way inside—"

"Yep." Dr. Morgan nodded.

Addison helped herself to food. "I think the calf is adorable. I want to be a veterinarian when I grow up." Dr. Morgan answered a few questions while he ate his sandwich and chips. When the others were done, I asked the question which had puzzled me at the time.

"What were you looking at on your phone?"

"And who did you call?" Dixie asked.

Dr. Morgan swallowed before answering. "I called my dad. He grew up on a farm and used to tell us stories about delivering cows and sheep." He wiped his mouth with a napkin. "He told me what I would have to do and then I watched a YouTube video."

"Isn't technology wonderful." B.J. drank her Coke. "You can find a video on practically everything."

When everyone was finished eating, we were ready to get down to business.

Dixie looked across at Addison. "Addison, can I trouble you to take the dogs for a walk?"

Addison hopped up and eagerly got the dogs leashed.

Beau rose. "Let me help you."

He and Addison secured all of the leashes and then headed outside.

When the door closed, B.J. wiped her mouth. "Well, I'll go first." She glanced around before she continued. "That chauffeur was halfway lit up before he even got into the tent for lunch. He keeps a flask in his jacket which he refills with liquor from the back of the limo."

Monica Jill banged her hand on the table. "Well, that's not right. He shouldn't be drinking and driving. That's just plain dangerous."

"Well, I certainly won't be riding with him," B.J. said. "He kept implying that he knew things about people."

"What sort of things?" Dixie asked.

She shrugged. "I never could get him to say. Trust me, I tried everything to get him to talk, but he just kept drinking from his flask and saying how *he knew things* and he was going to show them."

"Who's them?" I asked.

She shrugged. "He wouldn't say. He would just take a swig from the flask and grin." She shivered. "Anyway, he definitely knows something, but I couldn't get anything out of him."

Monica Jill raised her hand. "I'll go next if that's alright." She looked around.

We all nodded.

"I think Mary and Fergus are a nice couple, but boy are they hard to understand." She shook her head.

I glanced at Stephanie and stifled a laugh, but I wasn't quick enough to escape Monica Jill's notice.

She huffed. "Now, I know I have a bit of a southern accent."

"A bit," everyone said at once and then laughed.

She smiled and shook her head. "I don't know what y'all are talking 'bout. I sound just like you two." She pointed to Stephanie and me.

We exchanged glances and then shook our heads.

Monica Jill waved us off. "Well, I still say, those two are hard to understand with those thick Scottish accents."

"Which one of them was actually related to Lowry?" I asked.

"Mary said Lowry was her cousin." She shook her head. "Although, thankfully, I didn't see the slightest bit of a resemblance." She paused. "Where was I. Oh, yeah, Well, they asked a lot of questions about Tennessee and the dogs."

"Was this their first visit to America?" B.J. asked.

Monica Jill frowned. "Now, that's interesting. They said it was, but I got the distinct impression that maybe they'd been here before." She paused. "At least, it sounded like Fergus had."

"What made you think that?" I asked.

"We were talking about America and he mentioned something about Vegas that sounded like he'd been there once. I must have looked puzzled, because Mary said he had always wanted to go to Vegas and looked forward to going while they were here."

B.J. pursed her lips. "Maybe Fergus made a trip to Vegas without Mary. You know what they say, 'what happens in Vegas…'"

We shrugged.

Monica Jill sighed. "I have to say, I didn't really like Mary and Fergus and I got the distinct impression they think they'll inherit." She frowned. "I didn't want to disappoint them, but I think they have certain…expectations."

Stephanie shook her head. "They may have expectations, but from what I gathered from Eli, ah…Mr. Goldstein, it doesn't look like they'll be able to contest the will." She glanced at Monica Jill. "I'm sorry, were you done?"

"Oh yes. That's all I got. You go right on ahead." Monica Jill took a sip of her water.

"Eli didn't want to share the contents of Archibald Lowry's will, but he did say apart from a few legacies for the housekeeper, butler and a few others, the majority of his money was slated to go to various charities."

"Nothing for the cousins?" Dixie asked.

Stephanie shrugged. "Not that he mentioned. However, on Monday I can go and get a copy from the probate court."

Dr. Morgan raised his hand to go next. When he'd returned to check on the calf, he'd had a chance to talk to Mai. "Mai hasn't been on the estate long, but she mentioned there are some really strange things going on."

"Strange how?" Dixie asked.

"She said Archibald Lowry wanted her to sell the stock."

"What's unusual about that?" I asked. "I don't know anything about farms or animals, but surely people do that all of the time?"

Everyone nodded.

"He probably got in over his head with all of his Scottish Laird business," Stephanie said.

Dr. Morgan frowned. "That's what I said, but the weird thing is that he didn't want her to tell anyone she was selling them."

"Why would he do that?" I looked around.

Dixie shook her head.

Monica Jill frowned. "I've had people who want to buy land anonymously, because they're afraid the price will go up, but I've never heard of selling stock anonymously."

"Did she know if he was planning to move?" I asked.

Dr. Morgan shook his head. "Apparently Archibald Lowry wasn't forthcoming when it came to the hired help." He blushed. "I asked her out to dinner next week and I'll try to find out more then."

B.J. smiled. "Aww…shookie shookie."

Mr. Morgan's color deepened. "I'm merely trying to do my part toward the investigation."

"Of course, you are." Monica Jill smiled and gave his arm a squeeze. "I'm really happy for you. She's just the cutest little thing."

Dixie shared the incident we witnessed between the butler and chauffeur. We were going to try and get a word with the housekeeper before it was time to leave to get dressed for tonight's festivities.

I stood up and that's when someone outside screamed.

We rushed from the RV to see that a crowd had gathered near a portable john. We pushed our way past everyone only to see Paul Carpenter take a few steps, stumble forward and then collapse on the ground. Similar to Archibald Lowry, he had a large amount of blood around his chest.

Dr. Morgan pushed his way through the crowd, knelt down and felt for a pulse. After a few minutes, he shook his head. "He's dead."

Dixie placed her head in her hands. "Not again."

Chapter 11

By the time Red arrived on the scene, we had our hands full trying to keep people from leaving and still maintaining the integrity of the crime scene. Dixie, normally so calm cool and collected, was a nervous wreck. Not only was there a dead body blocking one of only two portable johns, but her big fundraising event was being ruined.

I looked at my friend's face as she sat at her RV dining table. "I'm sure everything will turn out okay in the end."

Dixie glanced in my direction. She was silent, but her face spoke volumes.

I reached across the table and gave her hand a squeeze. "Surely, no one will blame you for this."

She raised an eyebrow. "The buck stops here." After a few seconds, she laughed. "Buck...get it? All of the bucks for the poodle rescue are stopping here."

I squeezed her hand tighter. "No, they haven't. Now, pull yourself together or I might have to smack some sense into you the same way you did for me once."

She gave me a half-hearted smile. "Okay, Hercule. What do you have in mind?"

I didn't have anything in mind, so I sat up and forced my gray cells to get busy. "We know B.J. thought Paul Carpenter might be planning to blackmail someone." I turned to B.J. who nodded.

"Yeah, so what?" B.J. asked. "We don't know who."

I gave B.J. a sideways look that said *you're not helping.*

"Sorry." She picked up her coffee cup and took a sip.

Dixie sighed. "B.J.'s right. We don't have any idea who he was going to blackmail. We don't know anything."

Even though the comments were defeatist, they stimulated something in my brain. "We may not know specifically *who* he was planning to blackmail, but we can definitely narrow things down."

"How?" Dixie asked tentatively.

"B.J. said he mentioned he knew things about people." I turned to B.J. who nodded. "Well, that eliminates the majority of the people here today."

Monica Jill sat up straight in her chair. "That's right. It would have to be someone that he had already come into contact with."

I reached into my purse and pulled out a notepad and pen. "Let's write down our suspects."

B.J. leaned forward. "That shady looking butler would be at the top of my list."

"Ivan Bradington." I wrote his name on the paper.

Monica Jill glanced at Stephanie. "I'm not sure what was going on between him and that hunk of an attorney."

"Eli Goldstein." I resisted the urge to glance at Stephanie.

"I asked Eli about that," Stephanie said. "He said Carpenter was angry because he had some idea that Lowry was going to leave him a legacy in his will."

I glanced at Stephanie. "Did he?"

She shook her head. "Eli said Lowry left the chauffeur a couple thousand dollars, but apparently Carpenter was expecting more."

"What about the Kilpatricks?" Monica Jill asked. "He would have driven them around and he might have heard something." I added their names to the list. "He could have overheard them plotting to murder their cousin." I tapped my pen on the table. "I wonder if they're included in the will." I glanced at Stephanie.

She shrugged. "I'll know tomorrow. I don't want to ask Eli." She blushed. "You might as well go ahead and add his name to the list too."

I hesitated a half second and then added the lawyer to the list. "You're right. We can't eliminate anyone at this point in the game." I looked around and waited.

Dixie sighed. "We should put Mrs. Huntington on the list. I mean, she seems harmless enough, but…a little nervous."

"Wouldn't you be nervous if your boss and one of your coworkers were just murdered?" B.J. asked.

We looked at each other, but no one had a response to that. After a few moments, Dixie asked, "Who was that redheaded woman I saw you staring at before we went into the tent for lunch?"

"Fiona Darling." I wrote the name with a flourish. I explained how I'd met Fiona at the cocktail party.

Monica Jill frowned. "Just because she found Archibald Lowry's body doesn't mean that she knew him." She hesitated. "I mean, she might just be curious about dogs."

"That woman doesn't know a poodle from a Golden Retriever." I ignored the voice whispering in my head that just a few months ago, I barely knew the difference between the two breeds myself. I glanced up at Dixie and noticed the corners of her mouth twitching. "Don't even think about laughing at me."

Dixie hesitated a few seconds but then burst out laughing. It wasn't long before the others joined her. After a few seconds, I started laughing too. "Okay, I will admit that I might be just the tiniest bit jealous of her drop-dead gorgeous looks and mane of thick hair, but that doesn't mean she didn't kill Lowry and his chauffeur."

I think the laughter worked its magic. Dixie's cheeks had regained some of their color and her eyes were a little brighter.

I smiled at my friend. *"A merry heart doeth good like a medicine..."*
Dixie smiled. "Proverbs 17:22."

We chatted a bit longer. "Why do I feel like I'm missing someone or something?"

Monica Jill gasped. "Oh my God." She looked around with a sad expression. "We forgot Mai. Although I can't believe that petite little thing had anything to do with killing either one of those men." She shook her head. "Nope, I don't believe it."

"Petite doesn't mean weak." Dixie glanced around. "As a gamekeeper, I'm sure she's had to deal with a lot of animals and that requires strength."

I sighed and added Mai Nguyen to our list of suspects.

"Did you see the way Dr. Morgan blushed when he was talking about her?" Monica Jill asked.

We all nodded.

"It's just so cute."

"What's cute?"

I was so engrossed in our conversation and didn't hear Dr. Morgan enter the RV. I scrambled to cover the list of names with my arms without appearing to hide them. Based on the look his face, I knew I had failed.

He walked over to the table and slid the sheet of paper from under my arm. He looked at the sheet and I noticed a slight flush rise up the back of his neck. He placed the sheet back on the table, poured himself a cup of coffee and sat down without saying a word.

I tried to think of something to say to relieve the awkward silence, but nothing came to mind. I glanced at Dixie.

She picked up a sandwich and holding it like a carrot, she did a Bugs Bunny impersonation. "What's up, doc?"

Once again, we all laughed and the mood lightened.

"What can you tell us about Paul Carpenter's murder," I asked when we had composed ourselves.

"He was stabbed with a thin, sharp object," Dr. Morgan replied.

"Would a woman be able to do it?" I asked.

"I'll know for sure when I get the body to the morgue, but I'd say yes. It looks like it was caused by a really sharp blade, like a scalpel."

We talked for several minutes. When there was a lag in the conversation, Dr. Morgan cleared his throat. "Look, I know you're all thinking that I'm too close to one of the suspects to be objective." He colored. "However, I assure you that I am fully capable of doing my part to investigate this murder and will do everything in my power to bring the killer to justice." He coughed. "No matter who it is."

Everyone started talking at once in an effort to reassure him, but we stopped when he held up a hand.

"Thank you," Dixie said and reached across the table to pat the doctor's hand.

Each of us did a similar gesture of reassurance. After that was over, there was another awkward silence until B.J. broke it by asking, "Okay, now that the love fest is over, what's the plan?"

Everyone turned to me.

"We all have our suspects. I say we continue on. We each will question someone on the list and then we'll all meet after dog class on Tuesday and compare notes." I glanced around.

Everyone nodded except B.J. "Wait, my suspect is dead. I need someone else."

I looked down at the sheet. "I think you should tackle Fiona Darling. She's a private investigator." I looked at B.J. "Insurance companies hire private investigators sometimes, right?"

She nodded. "Oh yes. In fact, I have an arson claim that I need an investigator for now."

"Great, then it all worked out perfectly."

"What worked out perfectly?"

I nearly jumped out of my skin at Red's voice. "You scared me."

He stared. "Guilty conscience?"

Monica Jill got up and walked over to the cabinet. "Can I pour you a cup of coffee?"

B.J. slid the papers we'd been writing on under the table, folded them and slipped them over to me.

I felt Stephanie's hand touch my leg and I slid the papers to her.

"Please tell me I can have my silent auction?" Dixie pleaded.

Red shrugged. "You can have your auction."

Dixie's face lit up and she started to rise, but something in Red's manner stopped her.

"You can have your auction next week."

She flopped down.

His face softened. "I'm sorry, but we have an active crime scene here. Besides, I'm not sure it's safe to hold the auction tonight." He paused. "Give us some time to find this murderer. Just give me one week, okay?"

Dixie released a heavy sigh. "I don't suppose I have much choice."

Red smiled. "Actually, you don't but I appreciate your cooperation."

Addison and Beau entered the RV with the dogs. "We're getting pretty good at this." Beau smiled down at his new helper.

Addison held the two small poodles, Rex and Aggie, and gently placed them on the floor with the larger dogs.

The dogs crowded the water dishes that were placed in the kitchen area.

B.J and Dr. Morgan took their dogs and made a quick exit. Monica Jill, Addison and Jac were the next to leave and that reduced the noise and energy level in the RV instantly.

I turned to Beau. "How on earth did you two manage eight dogs at once?"

He smiled. "I'll have you know I'm a highly skilled dog wrangler." He chuckled. After a few minutes he added, "Addison and I decided to divide and conquer. The larger dogs are all fairly well-behaved, plus Chyna and Leia clip together." He held up a "Y" shaped leash. "They walked on one side, while Lucky walked on the other one. Addison took Jac and Snoball."

I was about to speak when Beau held up a hand. "Don't worry, we didn't forget Aggie and Rex." That's when he held up a backpack looking harness which allowed the dogs to fit in a pouch on his chest. "It's easier to wear the smaller dogs."

I smiled. "That's great, but what about Max?"

"Dr. Morgan took Max with him."

"If Addison was able to handle Snoball and Jac, then she's got some serious dog handling skills. That Jac is a handful," Dixie said.

He smiled. "Jac was the challenge. That dog has unlimited energy. For him, I had something special." He stepped outside. He hefted a large crate on a folding cart. There were bungee cords that secured the crate in place.

"That's ingenious." I stared.

Dixie smiled as she watched Beau fold the crate and cart flat and slide it into a closet. "I almost forgot we had that. There's so much equipment that you have to bring to dog shows that most competitors have something like that. Wheeled crates, stackable crates, and all kinds of wagons and other contraptions to help reduce the number of trips."

We chatted a bit longer. After a while, I turned to Red. "Are we free to go home?"

He nodded. "I know where to find you if I have questions." He kissed me briefly. Before he pulled away, he leaned close and whispered, "Be careful with your sleuthing."

I pulled away and tried to look as innocent as possible. "I have no idea what you're talking about."

"Look, I know I can't stop you, but I would be remiss in my duties as a law enforcement officer if I didn't at least warn you." He held my chin and looked me in the eyes. "Please, be careful. There's a murderer out there. He's killed twice and gotten away with it." He paused and caressed my cheek. "I don't want you to get hurt."

I nodded. "I'll be careful."

Dixie and Beau drove Stephanie and me home in the RV. I knew Dixie was disappointed that the auction had to be postponed. However, I had to admit it was nice to sit down and relax.

Stephanie and I ordered a pizza and ate it in on the back deck. It was getting dark, but I had bug lights and we burned a citronella candle to keep the mosquitos away. It was cool, but it felt nice to sit and enjoy each other's company.

We sat quietly and just enjoyed the silence together. It was good to have my daughter here. Stephanie had lived on her own for years, but whenever she came to visit, it felt like a comfortable sweater. We were able to sit in peace without feeling the need to fill the silence with words. The dogs played and ate and eventually curled up together on the deck and rested.

I watched their chests rise and fall and tried to remember what my life had been like before Aggie. That little dog had wiggled her way into my heart. When she looked up at me with those big brown eyes filled with love and adoration, I knew what unconditional love must feel like. I thought about my life when I was married to Stephanie's father, before he left me for an exotic dancer who was younger than our children. I couldn't remember what that was like. I don't mean I couldn't remember Albert. I remembered the house where we lived in Lighthouse Dunes. I remembered what he looked like. I remembered being there, but I couldn't recall peaceful moments like this where I was content and happy to sit and enjoy the silence. I couldn't remember feeling useful apart from cooking, cleaning and taxiing kids from drama class to debate club or soccer practice. I couldn't remember a time when I felt content and useful because of the work I was doing. I'm sure there must have been those moments, but I couldn't remember them. My life before moving to Chattanooga felt more like a movie reel. It was something I endured, not something I enjoyed. I thought about Red and tried to remember when Albert had looked at me like a man looks at a woman he truly cares about, but those looks, if they had ever existed, had floated away like the smoke from a citronella candle.

Stephanie sighed several times. After the third or fourth sigh I asked, "Is something bothering you?"

She shook her head. "No, actually I was just thinking how peaceful this is."

I smiled. "I was thinking the same thing."

"You seem so happy." She looked at me. "You have friends and Aggie." She glanced at the little dog sleeping on the deck and smiled. Then, she gave me a sly look. "And you've got Red."

I felt the heat rise up my neck. I squelched the smile that threatened to break out on my face and looked intently at my daughter. "Are you okay with...Red and me?"

She smiled and leaned across to squeeze my hand. "Absolutely. I like Red. He seems really nice and I love the way he looks at you."

I smiled. "I love that too. He makes me feel...special."

"You are special. Every woman should have someone that looks at them that way." She sighed.

"Does Joe make you feel special?"

She hesitated, but then she nodded. "He does." She laughed. "Sometimes, he's so serious and then he'll say or do something really sweet." She paused for a few moments and smiled as she obviously recalled a pleasant memory. "I had a really big case I was preparing for court and I'd been working all weekend on it. Joe was up visiting, but I didn't have a lot of time to spend with him. No complaints. He took Turbo and Lucky out to the park and cooked all of the meals. He even brought my meals in on trays to make sure I ate." She smiled. "I love strawberry shortcake and he tried several times to make it, but he kept forgetting ingredients. Something always seemed to go wrong. After the third failed attempt he left and took three trains

and a bus to Schaumburg to my favorite bakery and bought a shortcake."
She smiled at the memory.

"That's so sweet."

"He has his moments." She shook off the memory. "Then, there are
other times when I want to strangle him."

I didn't want to ruin the memory, but I had to ask. "What about Eli
Goldstein?"

She chuckled. "I don't know him well enough to strangle him."

"You know what I mean."

She took a sip of her wine and shrugged. "I just met him. He's very
handsome, but…I don't know. There's something about him that's just
too….well, too…"

"He's too handsome."

She nodded. "Yeah. I know it's wrong, but he just doesn't seem real to
me. I enjoy looking at him, but I can't imagine life with him. I can't picture
him in his designer suits and fifteen-hundred-dollar Italian leather shoes
cleaning up dog poop or rolling on the floor playing with two huge dogs
so I can prepare for court…or…"

"Or taking three trains and a bus to the suburbs to get strawberry
shortcake?"

She nodded. "Exactly."

We sat outside a bit longer until the candle began to burn out and then
we gathered our plates and glasses, roused the dogs and went inside.

Monday morning was a workday for me. I had been tempted to take
the day off and spend it with Stephanie, but I had some work I needed to
do in preparation for our taxes, an upcoming audit and the board meeting.
The previous night we agreed that Stephanie would drop me off at work so
she could keep the car and then she would meet me downtown for lunch.

Neither of us was keen on letting the dogs out alone so when I awoke, I
waited on the deck while the three dogs took care of their business before
I finished getting dressed.

It seemed like a month since I'd been to the museum, even though it was
only two days. I knew deep down inside that I wasn't to blame for Archibald
Lowry's murder, but I still felt guilty for talking Linda Kay into allowing
the Chattanooga Museum to host the event. I really enjoyed working at the
museum and didn't want to cause trouble. Guilt often translated into food
in my mind. So, I had Stephanie take me to DaVinci's, a bakery located
about one block from the museum.

"Bakery?" Stephanie glanced at the treats strategically placed in the shop window to entice passersby.

I glanced at my watch. "Why don't you park, and we'll go inside and see if we can snag a table and have a pastry and a coffee."

She glanced at the coffee in the cup holder she'd made at home and then turned the wheel and pulled into the lot beside the building. DaVinci's was a European style café located in the arts district of Chattanooga. In addition to house-roasted coffees, they offered an assortment of artisan breads, hand-dipped chocolates and delicious, hand-made pastries.

Inside, the smell of fresh brewed coffee, buttery pastries and sugary deliciousness crept into our noses and pulled us deeper into the bakery's lair. I watched Stephanie take a deep breath and inhale the glorious scent of sugar and coffee. She was hooked.

"Good morning, Mrs. Echosby. What can I get for you today?" Brad greeted me as he did most mornings. I discovered the bakery when I started working at the museum and had become a regular, stopping in practically every day.

I smiled. This must be what the regulars from the television show *Cheers* felt at a place where *everybody knew your name.* "Hello, Brad. I'll take a pastry box for work and how about a croissant and large coffee." I turned to Stephanie. "This is my daughter, Stephanie."

"You must be the lawyer from Chicago." Brad smiled. "Are you here visiting your mom?"

Stephanie nodded, but I could tell she was surprised this stranger knew so much about her. She quickly ordered a coffee and a pastry.

We were fortunate and found a seat at one of the small bistro tables near the window. When we were seated, Stephanie took a sip of her coffee. "Hmmm. This is delicious."

I smiled. It was nice to get to spend a few minutes with my daughter. I was very proud of her success, but I missed having time to just talk and enjoy each other's company.

"What?" She looked at me over her coffee.

"Nothing. I was just thinking how nice it is to spend time with you." I smiled. "I love Chattanooga, but I do miss you and David."

She reached out a hand and squeezed mine.

I shook off the mood and smiled. "But, you're here now and I'm going to enjoy as much time with you as possible." I stared. "You don't mind me going into the museum do you, because I'm sure Linda Kay—"

"Mom, of course I don't mind. You have work to do. My decision to come down for a visit at the last minute was unexpected. We'll have plenty of time to spend together."

"I plan to take off a few days later this week, but with the auditors coming to work on the financial statement and the upcoming board meeting, I just want to make sure that everything is done and ready."

She smiled. "Trust me, I completely understand about work and deadlines." She glanced out the window at the flowering trees and shrubs and sighed. "This is such a wonderful place. I can see why you like Chattanooga so much."

Something in her voice made me ask, "Are you considering leaving Chicago?" I tried to make sure my voice was neutral. Perhaps she was considering moving back to Light House Dunes to be with Joe.

She shrugged. "I don't know. I love what I do. I love the energy of Chicago. I just hate the traffic and the cold weather." She stared down into her coffee. "I want to have a family...someday, but I don't want to give up my career. I worked hard to get where I am and I'm not ready to just toss it aside to be a full-time wife and mother."

I listened carefully and when she finished, I took a deep breath. "I wish I knew the right words to say. I know women's magazines tell us we can have it all. They say you can have a career *and* a family. You can bring home the bacon *and* fry it up in a pan." I chuckled. "I'm sure there are plenty of women who have found the magic formula that allows them to achieve everything." I sighed. "I wasn't one of them. Your father didn't want his wife working. He wanted me home, raising the children and taking care of the family." I paused. "It was a choice I agreed to."

"Do you regret giving up your career to be a stay-at-home mom?"

I thought for a few minutes, but then smiled and shook my head. "I don't. It may have been your father's idea initially, but it was something I wanted to do. I wanted to be there for you and David. It was my choice." I smiled. "I think there are tradeoffs with everything in life. Only you can decide what is most important to you."

She looked up. "Thank you."

I looked puzzled. "For what?"

"For choosing to always be there for us."

I came very close to tearing up, so I swallowed hard and took a sip of my coffee.

We sat in a companionable silence for a few more minutes and then I said goodbye and took my box of pastries and walked the short distance to the museum.

Jacob was, as usual, already at his desk when I arrived. I placed the box on his desk as I passed. I brought pastries from DaVinci's at least two times per week, so he wasn't surprised by my edible offering and merely rose and took the pastries into Linda Kay's office.

Jacob had opened my office door and pulled the curtains in the window that looked out on the Tennessee River. I dropped my purse in the drawer and spent a couple of minutes enjoying the view and the peace and quiet of the early morning. After a few moments, there was a knock on my door.

"Linda Kay is here, if you'd care to join us," Jacob said.

I took a deep breath and prepared to face my boss.

Linda Kay Weyman's office was next to mine and enjoyed the same wonderful view of the Tennessee River. Her office was massive with room not only for a large desk but also a conference table and six chairs. "Hello, there. It sounds like you've had a busy weekend." Linda Kay smiled big. "Take a seat and tell me what happened."

Linda Kay Weyman was a middle-aged Southern Belle with thick red hair, bright eyes and a smile that came from the heart. She had one leg but never let that stop her from doing anything she set her mind to, whether it was career success or kick-boxing classes. At some point I would get up the courage to ask her how she managed that. However, today I was busy trying to gauge how much trouble Archibald Lowry's murder had caused.

"I'm so sorry about everything. I hope the board—"

Linda Kay held up a hand. "Now, you just let me worry about the board. I want to know what you've discovered." She gave me a sly smile. "I'm sure you've been investigating and I want to hear all of the juicy details."

Jacob poured tea into the tea cups he'd set out while Linda Kay helped herself to a strawberry tart and placed it on the blue and white porcelain plate.

Linda Kay had acquired a number of beautiful, and expensive, collections over the decades that she'd worked at the museum. Surprising to me, she believed in using rare china, crystal vases and art rather than putting them behind glass protective cases. In fact, the paintings on the walls of her office were authentic. I was still adjusting to someone who actually used her best items rather than storing them away. I grew up in a home where the good china, which wasn't even close in price to the plate I was eating from today, was kept locked up and only used once or twice per year, if at all. However, Linda Kay believed in using objects as their creator intended and enjoyed surrounding herself with beautiful things.

With care, I placed my teacup in its saucer and told Linda Kay and Jacob everything I knew about Archibald Lowry.

They listened with rapt attention. Jacob added a few bits from his experience on Friday night, but was silent when I discussed Saturday and Sunday. When I was finished, I waited.

Linda Kay smiled. "Well, that's fascinating. I can't wait to meet everyone on Saturday when the police have cleared the auction to be rescheduled."

I stared at her with wide eyes and an open mouth.

Linda Kay laughed. "Now, you can just close your mouth and stop looking surprised."

I complied, at least with closing my mouth. "You mean to say you're going to let Dixie have the auction here?"

She nodded.

"But what about the board?"

"Pshaw." She waved her hand as if flinging away an annoying gnat. "Dixon Vannover is an arrogant, pompous social climber who is just using the museum board as a stepping stone to advance his political career." She took a deep breath. "He's just a young pup who wants to bark all the time." She shook her head. "He likes to think he's a big shot." She sat tall and puffed out her chest, but then relaxed and smiled. "Well, I may not have a string of degrees, but I'm a lot smarter than he thinks." She leaned forward and winked at me.

"Well, how? What? I don't understand." I sputtered and stared from her to Jacob who was struggling to keep from laughing.

"Honey, I just phoned up a couple of my friends." She smiled. "They ran newspaper, radio and television ads that were incredibly favorable about the museum and our charitable work to help the poodle rescue."

Jacob smiled. "Linda Kay knows everyone. She's even friends with the governor."

I wasn't into politics, but I couldn't help being impressed. "You run in some impressive circles."

"I went to college in Alabama with his wife." She smiled. "We're sorority sisters, but I'm not showing Dixon all of my cards. I'm keeping that one up my sleeve for now." She gazed off as though she was seeing something in the future. After a few seconds, she nodded. "No, I think Dixon will try something and I want to be ready for him. Anyway, I didn't have to play my entire hand. Even though Archibald Lowry was murdered here, the publicity for the museum was all very positive. So, we're fine."

I leaned forward. "Are you sure? I was prepared to turn in my resignation if necessary."

She swatted away my response with a wave of her hand. "Oh no you won't. We have an audit and the annual report coming up." She smiled.

"Don't think you're going to get away with leaving Jacob and me to handle all that financial mumbo jumbo."

I knew Linda Kay understood more about finances than she was letting on, but I appreciated her support and leaned across and hugged her.

We sat and talked a bit longer. She was excited about the auction and was planning to come on Saturday to support the poodle rescue. I don't know why, but just knowing that Linda Kay would be present this time made me feel at ease.

When Linda Kay learned my daughter was here visiting, she was excited to meet her. I promised to introduce her when she picked me up for lunch.

We chatted a bit longer and then Jacob reminded Linda Kay she had a meeting in fifteen minutes. I left and Jacob cleared Linda Kay's office of all traces of our breakfast.

I spent the next few hours engrossed in spreadsheets and numbers. I'd gone over the figures so many times, I was sure I'd see them in my sleep. I was just about to check them once again when my phone started to vibrate.

It was a message from Stephanie letting me know she was downstairs.

I checked the time. I quickly responded that she should come up.

In less than five minutes, there was a light tap on my door. Jacob stuck his head in. "I found this young woman wandering the halls. She claims she is related to you?" He grinned, stepped aside and welcomed Stephanie into my office.

Stephanie entered and I made the introductions.

"I've heard my mom talk about you so much, I feel like I know you." She shook hands.

Jacob raised an eyebrow. "I'm not sure if that's good or bad, but I'm going to go with good." He smiled. "How long are you visiting?"

"Just a week. I leave Sunday."

"Well, we need to make sure you see all of the sights. Now, what did you see last time you were here?"

Stephanie and Jacob talked about the obvious attractions and then he provided a list of sights which he recommended that were off the typical tourist path. After a few moments, he checked his watch. "I think Linda Kay should be finishing her meeting now and I know she'd love to meet you."

He walked to Linda Kay's door, knocked and then entered.

Linda Kay had just finished a conference call and had a short window before her next meeting started. She waved Stephanie inside. She was gracious and complimented Stephanie on her beauty, welcomed her to Chattanooga and then encouraged me to take my laptop home and work from home the rest of the week so I could spend more time with my daughter.

I thanked her and promised we would spend as much time together as the work allowed. Her phone rang signaling her next meeting and we slipped out quietly.

There are a lot of wonderful restaurants in downtown Chattanooga, but when I asked if she had a taste for anything special, Stephanie requested a hamburger and milkshake from the dive Dixie had introduced us to on her last visit. So, we headed to the small diner.

The first time we'd eaten here, we thought Dixie was out of her mind. After we tasted the hamburgers and incredible shakes, we understood the attraction.

She'd proclaimed them the "Best greasy burgers and shakes you'll ever eat," and she was right.

There were only about ten tables in the entire restaurant, so we counted ourselves lucky when a couple left as we arrived. We hurried and secured our seats. A middle-aged man with a bald head and long beard and mustache came to the table to take our orders. He was wearing jeans and a T-shirt. Every inch of exposed skin was covered in tattoos. He placed napkins and a knife down for each of us.

"What can I get you ladies?" He smiled big.

We ordered fried cauliflower, hamburgers and milkshakes. It didn't take long before he returned and we were able to tuck into our food with zeal.

Stephanie sucked on her chocolate Shock-o-matic and squeezed her eyes and shivered as the brain freeze hit. After a few seconds, when she was able to talk, she said, "That has to be the best thing I've ever tried in my life."

I smiled. "You haven't tried the Cat-man-du." I slid my glass over and allowed her to taste the cashew and Himalayan pink salt burger, which was my personal favorite.

She took a sip and her eyes widened. "That's amazing."

I nodded.

We enjoyed our food in silence and once our appetites were sated, we sat back and allowed the grease and ice cream to settle.

There was a large envelope sticking out of the top of Stephanie's bag. "What's that?" I pointed.

"I almost forgot." She picked up the envelope and pulled out the papers inside. "Archibald Lowry's last will and testament." She slid it across to me.

I glanced at the document and tried to make sense of the legal language, but after a bit, I handed it back. "Maybe you could give me the Cliff Notes version."

She chuckled as she took the document. "He's left small legacies to his staff." She glanced through the document. "However, after his debts have been paid, the bulk of his estate and holdings are to be sold. The proceeds are to be distributed among various charitable organizations."

Something in her eyes made me suspicious. "I don't suppose there's anything wrong with that. Dixie mentioned he was interviewing various charities, which is why she met with him."

"I'm not saying there's anything suspicious about his decision to leave his money to charity. Lots of philanthropic minded people do that." She hesitated. "Did Archibald Lowry mention to Aunt Dixie that he planned to leave the bulk of his wealth to the Eastern Tennessee Poodle Rescue?"

I stared. "You're joking?"

She shook her head.

"How much is it?"

Stephanie looked around to make sure we weren't overheard and then leaned across the table and whispered, "I did a little research at the library while I was waiting, and we're looking at close to a half-billion."

I nearly choked. "Did you say, billion, with a B?"

She nodded.

"Good gracious." I stared at Stephanie. "I wonder if anyone has told Dixie."

We stared at each other for several seconds while I tried to get my mind around figures that large.

"Is it legal?" I asked.

Stephanie nodded. "It all appears to be in order."

There was something in her voice that worried me. "What's bothering you?"

She shook her head. "I don't know. It's just a bit...odd." She passed the document back to me. "Archibald Lowry intended to leave the bulk of his estate to the Scottish Heritage Foundation until a week ago. Look at the date." She pointed. "Something happened in the last week that made him change his mind."

"I wonder what happened?" I asked.

She shrugged. "No idea, but whatever it was, it must have been major because it cost the Scottish Foundation a fortune."

I stared at the will and then at my daughter. "That much money could make someone desperate."

She stared. "I'd love to know what happened to make Archibald Lowry withdraw such a large donation to a cause that was very close to his heart."

I sighed. "And, I wonder...."

She must have read my mind because she finished my thought by saying, "If losing that much money made someone angry enough to kill."

Chapter 12

"People have killed for a lot less." I thought for a few moments and then added, "Although, we shouldn't jump to conclusions."

Stephanie's phone rang. She answered and a slight flush rose in her cheeks. Even before she spoke his name, I knew she was talking to Eli Goldstein. Her flush was soon replaced with a scowl. "Well, I don't know, but I'll definitely ask her."

Listening to one side of a conversation was like trying to complete a crossword puzzle with only the across or down clues, but not both. So, I slurped the remains of my milkshake and waited. Thankfully, I didn't have to wait long.

Stephanie hung up and stared at me. "Well, that was strange."

"Strange how? Did he ask you out to dinner?"

"Yes, but that's not the strange part." She halted and shook her head. "That didn't come out right, but you know what I mean." She took a deep breath. "The strange part is that he said he talked to Mary and Fergus Kilpatrick. Apparently, they noticed how attached you were at the dog show to little Indulf." She glanced at me.

"Rex. I changed his name."

She nodded. "Well, they want to make you an offer for the dog."

I wasn't expecting that. "An offer?"

"According to him, they want Indulf…ah, Rex as a memorial of their cousin." She paused and watched my face.

"He's a dog, not a floral arrangement." I could feel my blood pressure rising. "He's a living, breathing, being with a personality, and he's *not* for sale."

Stephanie reached across the table and clasped my hands. "I know, but wait. Don't you want to know how much they're offering."

"No. No, I don't. It doesn't matter how much. He's not for sale."

She paused and I could tell she was itching to tell me. "Okay, how much?"

"Fifty-thousand dollars."

"You have got to be joking."

She shook her head slowly. "According to Eli, they could tell that you're attached and well, they wanted to provide significant compensation...or..."

I waited. "Or, what?"

"He implied that as the only living relatives of Archibald Lowry, they might take legal action, but hoped it wouldn't come to that."

My heart raced and I felt light headed as the blood rushed to my head. "Legal action? They're threatening me with legal action? Well, they can just bring it on. Rex is my dog and I'm not giving him up without a fight." I huffed.

Stephanie squeezed my hands. "I know."

I took several deep breaths and remembered that Stephanie was just the messenger. I gave her hands a squeeze. "I'm sorry, dear. I know this isn't your fault."

She gave a half smile. "It's okay. I know how you feel." She sat quietly and swallowed hard. "I remember how I felt when I first found Lucky. We bonded at once and then...that man wanted to take him." She batted away tears.

"Oh honey, I'm sorry." I felt the tears roll down my face, but I didn't bother to wipe them away.

Stephanie looked up and gave a nervous laugh. "We look a hot mess." She grabbed her napkin and wiped her face.

I rummaged in my purse until I found some tissues and pulled them out and did the same.

Stephanie wiped away most of her eye makeup, and her eyes were red from crying, but she still looked beautiful. I knew from past experience I wasn't a pretty crier and would need to reapply my makeup.

Our waiter tentatively approached our table. "Is everything okay? I hope there was nothing wrong with the food or the service?"

He looked so sincere that we both chuckled as we hastily reassured him that both the food and the service were fine.

After he left, Stephanie looked at me. "That poor man may never be the same."

We collected our belongings and prepared to leave. Stephanie hesitated before I rose. "Mom, I'm not familiar with Tennessee law, but I'm going to look into it. Legally, I don't believe they're entitled to him. They weren't listed as heirs and therefore, don't inherit, but I need to do some additional research. Regardless, I'll do what I can to make sure you don't lose Rex."

I nodded. "I know you will." I stood up.

"I'm also going to dinner with Eli Goldstein."

I started to speak, but the look in her eyes halted my words. "I think he knows something and I'm going to find out what."

Chapter 13

A quick search on her cell phone showed Stephanie the location for the nearest legal library. I'm a big fan of libraries, but I preferred the ones with a large mystery section. Thankfully, I got a text message from Dixie saying she was downtown, so I quickly arranged for her to pick me up.

Today Dixie was driving her Lexus rather than the RV, which meant she didn't have the poodles with her. I slid into the passenger seat and fastened my seat belt. "Where to?"

She eased into traffic and made a few turns which took her onto the interstate. "Back to Lowry's house. I want another chat with that butler."

"Good. I didn't get to talk much to the housekeeper. She seemed terrified, even before the chauffeur was killed."

"Well, her boss had been murdered recently, so…maybe she had a good reason for being frightened."

"Maybe, but…"

"But you don't believe it." Dixie headed up the mountain.

I told her about the offer by the Kilpatricks, via Stephanie, during the drive.

"Fifty thousand dollars? Are you joking?"

I shook my head. "Not according to Eli Goldstein. Are poodles worth that much money?"

She shook her head. "I've never heard of anyone paying that much money for one. Thoroughbred horses, yes. Dogs…no."

"Maybe the Kilpatricks will be at the house and I can find out why they're offering so much for him. I mean, they barely knew Archibald Lowry." I glanced at my friend. "Speaking of money did you know

Archibald Lowry left the Eastern Tennessee Poodle Rescue a large amount of money in his will?"

She smiled. "Really, that's nice. I knew he was looking at several charitable organizations, but I didn't know he'd chosen us."

I could tell from her calm response she had no idea of the amount. I turned in my seat to make sure I didn't miss her reaction when she found out how much. I needn't have bothered. When she heard the amount, she nearly drove off the side of the road.

She gave the steering wheel a sharp turn to the left and got the car back on the pavement. "Holy mother of God."

"I had a feeling you didn't know."

"Didn't know? Are you joking? I didn't have a clue. If I'd known, I wouldn't have been so stressed out about the silent auction." She shook her head. "That doesn't make any sense. Why would he do something like that. He barely knew me."

"I guess you must have made a big impression."

She shook her head. "No. I couldn't have made that much of an impression." She whistled. "That's just crazy."

"You said he was eccentric."

"I know, but…that's beyond eccentric."

"Maybe it just seems like a lot of money to us, but it wasn't that big of a deal to him. You know, everything is relative."

During the ride to Lowry's estate, we discussed a plan of action and a cover story for our presence. By the time Dixie pulled in front of the grand estate, we were both ready.

Archibald Lowry's estate was a large stone fortress with a circular driveway. Flying from a flagpole in front of the stone structure was the national flag of Scotland. Royal blue with a diagonal white cross called a saltire, the flag announced to all visitors the allegiance of the owner. The flag and the sheep which grazed in the front yard were two of the prominent features I remembered from my other visit.

We walked to the front door and rang the bell. After a short wait, we were greeted by Bradington.

"Hello, Bradington." Dixie pulled out her contract. "I wanted to go over a few things from the weekend to make sure everything is accurate and taken care of."

Bradington stood his ground, and for a split second it looked as though he wasn't going to allow entry. However, after an awkward few seconds during which Dixie flashed her biggest smile, he stepped aside and we entered.

The outside of the castle was dark and hard with a stone façade which was cold and uninviting. The interior was much the same. The gray interior stone walls lining the entry were softened slightly with massive tapestries depicting brutal scenes of stag hunting. We were led into a living space which continued the drab theme from the exterior. The living room was a manly, lumberjack's dream filled with dark wood from top to bottom. A massive stone fireplace dominated one of the walls. The stones appeared to have been taken from the same quarry as the stone that comprised the exterior with an opening large enough for a man to walk into. The room was dark with wood paneled walls, dark hard wood floors, and oversized dark wood furniture. Covering one of the wood paneled walls were deer and elk heads mounted on wood plaques. I tried not to stare, but found it difficult, especially at a wall of glass-eyed heads which all appeared to be staring at me.

Dixie focused on Bradington. "Now, where should we set up?"

"Excuse me?"

She patted her large purse. "I brought my laptop. It'll be a lot easier to just show you everything online." She glanced around. "Is there a table where I can spread out?"

Bradington sighed. "Follow me."

As the two headed through a doorway, I coughed. "Could I trouble you for a glass of water?" I smiled, but then remembered I was supposed to be choking and so I started coughing more loudly.

Bradington halted. "Certainly, I'll just go—"

"I don't want to bother you. I'm sure if you point me in the right direction, I can just nip in the kitchen and get it myself or maybe Mrs. Huntington…"

He hesitated a second but then pointed. "If you go through the dining room, you'll find Mrs. Huntington in the kitchen."

I nodded and hurried off, coughing for good measure as I walked. I looked around behind me but Bradington wasn't following.

The kitchen was small compared to the other rooms of the house. Terracotta floors, dark wood cabinets and appliances which were probably older than my children, based on the colors. Avocado green hadn't been popular since the early seventies.

I found Catherine Huntington sitting at a wood kitchen table, sipping tea. She was a large boned woman with a plain face, gray hair pulled back in a severe looking bun and the start of a moustache.

She started to rise when she saw me, but I held out a hand to stop her.

"Please don't get up. I was just hoping to get a glass of water." I looked around and saw an open shelf with tea cups. I pointed. "Would you mind if I joined you?"

She shrugged.

I hurried over and grabbed a teacup then sat down across from her. She poured tea from a brown betty teapot into my mug and we sat sipping our tea in a companionable silence for several minutes.

"You probably don't remember me, but my name is Lilly—"

"I remember you," she said in a gruff voice. "You were with that posh lady at the dog show."

I nodded. "That's my friend, Dixie."

She grunted and sipped her tea.

I glanced around the kitchen which was clean and tidy. "Have you worked for Mr. Lowry long?"

"Nigh on twenty-five years."

"That's a long time to work for the same person." I paused waiting for her to agree or disagree. She merely grunted and took another sip of tea.

"You must have enjoyed working here to have stayed so long."

"Yah."

I waited, but she was the queen of brevity.

"Have you enjoyed meeting Mr. Lowry's cousins? It must be nice having another woman in the house."

Catherine Huntington grasped the crucifix she wore around her neck and the medallion. At close proximity, I was able to make out the image on the medallion was that of St. Martin.

"Of course, having two more mouths to feed must be challenging."

She shrugged.

"Did you travel to Scotland often with Mr. Lowry?"

"Often enough."

"Is that where he met his cousins, Mary and Fergus Kilpatrick?" I smiled. "That must have been nice, a big family reunion in Scotland."

She started and sloshed tea on the table. The same look of fear that I'd noticed at the lunch flashed across her face but quickly vanished, replaced with the vacant look she'd worn earlier.

She got up from the table and got a towel to clean up the spilled tea.

I offered to help but was brushed away with a wave of her hand.

"Excuse me." She took her tea mug to the sink and started to wash it. "Ain't got time for gossip."

I felt the heat rush up my neck. Embarrassed, I rose, placed my cup on the counter and turned to leave. However, before I reached the door, I turned and walked back to Mrs. Huntington. "Listen, I don't want to get you in trouble, but maybe I can help."

She looked at me. "What do you mean?"

"I couldn't help but notice your medallion." I reached out and touched her arm.

Catherine Huntington jumped. "I don't know what you mean."

I gazed at her. "It's okay. I just want to help."

She closed her eyes and took several deep breaths. Then, as though a flood gate had been lifted, she said, "I ain't had no peace since the day Mr. Lowry was murdered and I don't expect to have any until I leave this house." She dropped her head. "I've done for Mr. Lowry for over twenty-five years and now the house is to be sold." Tears streamed down her face. "I'm too old to start over. No one will hire an old woman. Most folks don't want or need a live-in housekeeper and cook and I don't know how to do nothing else."

I patted her arm. "Don't worry. I'm sure we'll be able to find you a new position." Even though I already knew the answer, I asked, "Did Mr. Lowry leave you a legacy in his will?"

She grabbed a handkerchief and wiped her eyes. "Bless his soul, he left me five thousand dollars, but that won't buy me a place to live. If I do find another position, it'll likely not be a live-in. I'll have to make my way back and forth and that'll be expensive."

"Who told you about your legacy in Mr. Lowry's will?"

She sniffed. "Mr. Eli come by and told me. He was concerned and didn't want me to worry. Bless his soul."

I assured Catherine Huntington that I'd do my best to help her find another position and she cried tears of joy. I was just going to ask her again about Mary and Fergus Kilpatrick, when the two appeared in the kitchen doorway.

Mrs. Huntington immediately turned back to the sink and assumed her mask of a sullen faced domestic.

"Hello, it's Mrs. Echosby, isn't it?" Mary Kilpatrick smiled and spoke in her thick Scottish brogue.

Catherine Huntington grunted and turned back to the sink.

Mary Kilpatrick smiled. "Poor dear, nervous as a hare." She turned to me. "Now, what brings you here?"

"My friend, Dixie, had to go over some things with Mr. Bradington."

Fergus frowned. "Now, that wee lass should na' be talkin' to the butler." He puffed up his chest. "She should be talkin' to me or me wife. After all, if it's business she needs to discuss, that should be done with the laird."

He smiled, but it looked menacing and I shuddered involuntarily. He reached out a hand and touched my arm. "Now, I think you and I have a little business to discuss too."

I searched my brain but couldn't figure out what he and I could have to discuss when Mary Kilpatrick filled in the missing pieces.

"That wee pup is just the most darlin' thing and I know you've got your heart set on keepin' it." She gave a pouty smile.

Fergus was more forceful. "You may 'ave wanted ta keep it, but he belonged to me cousin Archie and I just know he'd have wanted him to stay in the family."

Before I could respond, Dixie entered the kitchen. "Lilly Ann, there you are."

"Yes, oh right Dixie. I have to go now, but I'll definitely keep what you've said in mind. We'll talk later."

I picked up my purse from the table and pulled Dixie, not so gently, toward the door.

Dixie nodded to Fergus and Mary and I waved a hasty good-bye as we high tailed it out of the house as quickly as possible.

We didn't speak until we were in the car and heading down the mountain.

"Are you going to tell me what that was about?" Dixie asked.

Dixie drove in silence while I told her all that happened with Fergus, Mary and Catherine Huntington. Kind hearted soul that she was, she immediately latched onto Mrs. Huntington's plight. "Well, I don't see a problem finding her a job." She paused while she navigated a sharp turn. "I mean, Beau and I could probably use some help around the house and our home is certainly big enough for her to live there."

I grinned. "I was hoping you'd say that."

She glanced at me and smiled. "Even though it's just Beau and me, we have Chyna and Leia and...I thought once I retired from showing, there would be plenty of time for cooking and cleaning, but now that I'm a judge I still go to just as many dog shows as before." She sighed. "Plus, there's my dog classes and the poodle rescue, and I'm still on three other boards." She shook her head. "There just doesn't seem to be enough time in the day."

I took a deep breath. "I think it would be great if you could take Mrs. Huntington, but there is something you should know."

She gazed at me from the corner of her eye. "Okay."

"I think she may be an alcoholic."

"Oh dear." After a few moments, she said, "What makes you think that? Don't tell me she was drunk."

"No, but I was thinking back to the luncheon, and remember when we drank to Archibald Lowry, well she didn't. I noticed that her hand was shaking a bit and she didn't drink her champagne."

"Maybe she doesn't like champagne."

"Have you noticed that she always seems to be clutching the crucifix and the medallion around her neck?"

Dixie nodded. "I assumed it's a Catholic thing."

"It is…sort of. Anyway, I got a good look at the image on the medallion and it's St. Martin of Tours."

"Who's St. Martin of Tours?"

"He's the patron saint of alcoholics."

"Oh." She drove on in silence for a few moments. "I don't know. Beau and I have alcohol in the house, and I wouldn't want to tempt someone who is struggling with an addiction."

"I understand, although I noticed Archibald Lowry had a bar."

"Good point. I'll talk to Beau and I'll let you know about the job."

I nodded.

"Now, what's the deal with the cousins? You dragged me out of that house so fast, you 'bout gave me a case of whiplash."

I related the conversation I'd had with the two Kilpatricks.

Dixie was clever and picked up on the one thing that had bothered me from the conversation. "Well, isn't that interesting. Fergus told you Archibald Lowry was his cousin when Mary told Monica Jill he was her cousin."

"Exactly."

"Either they have some strange familial relationships in that family… or…"

I nodded. "Or, one…or both of them is lying."

The remainder of the ride home was uneventful. When we pulled into the driveway, I recognized Red's truck in the driveway. When I didn't see him in the truck, I knew he was probably around the back sitting on the deck.

Dixie said, "I should go home, but I'm anxious to hear if Red found out anything more about the murders."

We went inside and Dixie went out back while I stopped at my bedroom. When I opened the door, Aggie and Lucky flew out of the room and raced down the hall to the back door. I stopped by the small crate where Rex was anxiously turning around in circles and pawing at the door. I opened the door and quickly scooped him up so he wouldn't squat before I got him outside and raced to follow Aggie. At the back door, I was surprised to see that Red and Dixie weren't alone. I opened the door and both dogs raced past me and down the steps where they began a quick round of chase with Red's dog, Steve Austin, followed closely by their Plott Hound buddy, Turbo.

"Joe, what a pleasant surprise. I didn't know you were coming."

He stood up when he saw me and we hugged.

Joe had been friends with Red in the military. In fact, Joe introduced Red to Stephanie and me when I first moved and ran into a bit of trouble at my previous rental. We met Joe when he was helping to investigate the murder of my husband, Albert. He was also my daughter's boyfriend, at least until recently.

Joe was a member of the Lighthouse Dunes K-9 division and rarely went anywhere without his partner, Turbo. Aggie was shamelessly enamored with Turbo and had stopped running and was now rolling in the grass with her dog friends. Rex leapt onto Turbo and nipped at him, anxious to join the fun.

Joe looked on anxiously and then whistled. Turbo stopped instantly and ran to him. Aggie and Rex followed. "Cute puppy. Whose is he?" He glanced from me to Dixie.

She pointed at me.

He smiled. "He's pretty tiny. Aggie is used to Turbo, but I don't want this little guy to get hurt."

Dixie waved him off. "Honestly, I think he'll be okay. I've been watching and Turbo is careful."

He smiled. "Aggie seems to like running with the big dogs."

I looked down at Aggie who was now trying to regain Turbo's attention. "The little hussy knows exactly what she's doing."

I leaned over and kissed Red, noticing the cooler beside him. "What's inside?" I asked.

"I brought some steaks and beer. If you haven't already eaten."

"Sounds good to me. Just let me change into some comfortable clothes." I turned to go inside. "You know where everything is."

I hurried to my bedroom and changed into a pair of jeans and a comfortable shirt. I stopped in the kitchen and got a head of lettuce from the fridge, quickly chopped it and put it in a large bowl along with tomatoes and cheese. I grabbed a bag of croutons and two bottles of salad dressing.

Red entered the kitchen while I was working. "Was it okay that I brought Joe?

"Of course. Joe is a friend. He's always welcome."

"I hear there's some...turbulence between him and Stephanie." He waited, but I didn't fill in the silence.

"Can you grab the silverware?" I said instead

He reached in the drawer and picked up the tray with the silverware.

Dixie and Joe were sitting at the table drinking beers and watching the dogs play in the yard. We chatted about dogs, Lighthouse Dunes, the weather and everything except the things that we most wanted to discuss, while Red manned the grill. He didn't take long and we were all comfortably eating steaks, roasted corn and salad while the dogs gobbled down a mixture of dry dog food mixed with grilled hot dogs.

Dixie kept giving me wide-eyed looks, sudden head tilts in Red's direction and eventually a kick to the shins which made my eyes water. When I was able to speak clearly, I asked, "Any progress on the murders?"

Red glanced up from his food. "Progress, yes." He took a drink. "Have we caught the killer, no."

Once the door was opened, Dixie burst through. "What progress have you made?"

Red gave Joe a look that said, *help me.*

Joe merely shrugged. "You might as well tell them what you know. They're going to go sleuthing with or without you."

Dixie reached across and patted Joe's arm. "That's very smart and you're absolutely right."

"Besides, we might have some information that could help." I flashed my best smile.

Red leaned forward. "You both realize withholding information is a criminal offense, right?"

I smiled. "I'm more than willing to cooperate with law enforcement."

He glared for a few seconds. Then he released a deep breath. "What the heck. Frankly, we haven't learned a lot, except..."

Dixie and I both leaned forward. "Except?"

"Except that no one seems to know where Archibald Lowry got his money and the best we can tell is that he's running some kind of second chances employment service."

Dixie and I exchanged glances. The puzzled expression on her face mirrored what mine must have looked like.

"What do you mean? Wasn't he a businessman?" Dixie asked.

Red nodded. "Yes, but when he first entered the business world, he seemed to already have quite a bit of money." He shrugged. "We've got our newest addition to the bureau working on it."

Something in his voice made me curious. I stared at him and then the reality dawned on me. "Madison?"

He nodded.

I hopped up from my seat, came behind him and gave him a big hug. "I'm so glad. That's great. David will be so excited."

Madison Cooper was a beautiful young woman we'd met a few months ago. She was great with dogs and had made a lasting impression with my son, David, who had been here visiting. I believe they were still on quite friendly terms. At least, I hoped so. David lived in New York City where he was a highly successful actor who traveled the world performing. I was glad for anything, or anyone, that would entice him to come down for a visit.

Madison had a unique set of skills which had landed her in trouble in her younger days. She was an adept Internet hacker, but thanks to Red she would now be able to use her skills for good.

"When does she start?" I went back to my seat. "I can't believe neither she nor David told me."

Red held up a cautionary hand. "She just found out today and we started her immediately." He rubbed the back of his neck. "We're short staffed at the moment, which is the only reason I was able to get her in. Normally, the process takes months."

"How—"

He held up a hand. "And she is only on probation. Her record as a juvenile would normally have prevented her from consideration, but," he shrugged, "she was really young when she was hacking and she didn't do anything black hat, so…"

After a few minutes, I recalled my son, David, explaining that *black hat* hackers got into systems for their own personal gain or malicious reasons. "I'm glad they were willing to give her a second chance."

"Seems to be a lot of that going around." Red leaned forward. "Archibald Lowry was running a second chances program all by himself."

"What do you mean?" Dixie asked.

"Everyone Archibald Lowry employed was an ex-con."

Dixie looked dumbstruck and if my face looked remotely as shocked as hers then I'd say the feeling was mutual.

"But…how? I mean who?"

"The butler, Ivan Bradington did time for robbery and murder. The chauffeur, Paul Carpenter, did a few years for extortion—"

This time it was my turn to interrupt. "What about Mrs. Huntington?"

He nodded. "Vehicular homicide."

I stared. After a few moments, Dixie reached over and closed my jaw.

Red merely shrugged. "Apparently, the housekeeper had a bit of a drinking problem." He shook his head. "She was so upset afterward, she had to go to a mental institution before she could even serve time. The judge was lenient and gave her three years."

Dixie turned to me and in her best Oliver Hardy voice said, *"Well, Stanley, here's another nice mess you've gotten me into."*

This time, Joe and Red exchanged glances. After a few moments, Red asked, "Are we missing something?"

In as few words as possible, I shared the conversation I'd had with Mrs. Huntington and that Dixie was considering hiring her.

Simultaneously, Joe and Red both said, "NO."

Red pinched his nose and I knew a lecture was coming. Instead, he appealed to Joe. "Maybe you can explain to them why this is such a bad idea."

Joe shook his head. "He's right. These people are murder suspects and... at least two of them are actually convicted murderers. You can't just invite them into your house."

I shook my head. "I know. I know, but she seemed so nice."

"I've read reports that Lizzie Borden's neighbors said the same thing about her," Red said.

In the distance, a loud boom of either a car backfiring or the sound of fireworks filled the air.

The sound startled Steve Austin, Red's pit bull/Labrador mix. The dog, which had moments earlier been standing by Red's side, climbed into his lap.

The sixty-pound dog quivered on his owner's lap with both paws wrapped around his neck.

Red tried to extract himself. "Some watchdog this is supposed to be."

Dixie cooed. "The poor dog."

Red glanced around the shivering animal. "Poor dog? He's afraid of everything." He patted the dog. "I thought pit bulls were supposed to be fierce."

Dixie clicked her tongue. "Pit bulls are one breed that gets a bad rap. Bad people train them for dog fights and make them vicious, but most pit bulls are loving, wonderful dogs." She reached out a hand and rubbed the quivering dog. "Is he like this whenever he hears loud noises?"

Red nodded. "Thunderstorms, car door slams, loud sounds on television."

"You might want to consider a Thundershirt."

"What's that?" he asked.

"It's a tight vest-like garment that can sometimes help with anxiety." She spoke in the teaching voice she used in her obedience classes. "If that doesn't work, you might want to talk to your vet about CBD oil."

Red's eyes widened. "You're joking, right?"

She shook her head. "Actually, there are a lot of studies that show it's extremely helpful in reducing canine anxiety."

We chatted for a few moments about dog anxiety treatment and then returned to our previous conversation.

Red narrowed his eyes. "What else have you been up to?"

We gave him a quick run-down on what we'd learned so far.

Dixie gasped. "Please tell me his gamekeeper, Mai Nguyen, hasn't murdered anyone." She clutched her hands over her heart. "I think Dr. Morgan has a crush on her and I'm sure it would break his heart."

"Small Asian woman with a big British accent and attitude?" Red asked.

I struggled to keep from laughing and nodded.

He shook his head. "She's just about the only one without a criminal record, but maybe I need to run a search on Interpol. I restricted my research to the United States."

"Yes. I think that would be a great idea." I sat up straight.

Dixie swatted my arm. "Are you crazy? Whose side are you on?"

"I was thinking if he ran a search on the Interpol database, he could track Mary and Fergus Kilpatrick."

Dixie relaxed. "Oh."

We both turned to stare at Red.

"I don't need to run them through Interpol." He paused and I could tell by the way his lips twitched, he was trying to avoid smiling. After a long pause, he said, "I don't have to run American citizens through Interpol."

"I think I'm going to need something stronger than this bottled water." I turned to Joe. "Can you hand me a pop from the cooler please?"

Joe reached down and handed me a Diet Coke.

Dixie stared at me with an odd expression on her face.

"What's wrong?" I popped the tab and took a long swig.

She swatted my arm again. "That's it. That's what was bothering me about the Kilpatricks."

"They drink Diet Coke?"

"No, it's the fact that you just asked for a pop."

I shrugged. "That's what we call it in the Midwest....well, at least in Indiana."

She looked at me. "Remember when we were in Scotland? People from different areas of Scotland had certain words that were unique. Just like in the United States."

I smacked the side of my head. "You're right."

Red and Joe exchanged looks. Finally, Red said, "I've never been to Scotland. Can one of you tell us what's going on?"

This was Dixie's revelation, so I nodded for her to explain. She took a deep breath and started talking slowly and calmly. "You know how in the United States, there are regional dialects. People here say *soda* or *soda pop*, where people from Indiana might say *pop?*"

Red and Joe both nodded.

"Well, Scotland was the same. People in Glasgow had different dialects and used different words than people in Edinburgh and...well, Shetland."

Red nodded again. "Okay, and...?"

"That's what bothered me about the Kilpatricks. Their accents seemed to be a mish-mash. There was no distinct dialect and the words were from all over the country." She shook her head. "It just sounded wrong...like...I don't know." She turned to me.

"It was like someone from the South trying to talk like a New Yorker or someone from Boston...It was exaggerated."

Joe nodded. "I think I get what you're saying."

Red nodded as well. "Well, your instincts were right. Mary and Fergus Kilpatrick are from Kansas City."

"Interesting, that Archibald Lowry's Scottish cousins are both from the United States." Red's phone rang and he stepped away to answer.

Dixie excused herself to visit the bathroom, leaving Joe and I alone at the table. Well, as alone as two people who were surrounded by five dogs could be.

Joe took a drink. "Will she be upset that I'm here?"

I didn't need to ask who 'she' was. I merely shrugged. "I don't know."

He nodded. "Red told me about the two murders and...I was worried." He leaned forward and ran his hands through his hair which he wore clipped in a short buzz cut that helped to identify him as a policeman. "I shouldn't have come."

I wasn't sure how to answer, but before I could, I heard voices inside and knew that Stephanie was home, and she wasn't alone.

Stephanie came to the back door. "Mom, we went to—"

Joe stood up as Stephanie stepped down onto the deck.

"Joe? What are you doing here?"

I was determined to stay out of this battle, but I noticed the color go up Joe's neck and a vein throb at the side of his head.

"Stephanie, isn't it wonderful that Joe was able to come down to help Red...with...well." For the life of me I couldn't think of what Joe was going to help with, so I merely waved my hand and hoped she wouldn't notice. "And he brought Turbo."

Lucky and Turbo were both on their back legs, vying for Stephanie's attention.

Eli stepped out onto the deck. Like a male model who just stepped off the pages of *GQ* magazine, he dominated the scene. His thick wavy hair was loose today and floated gently in the breeze. The first two buttons of his silk shirt were open exposing a very well-tanned chest and his muscular physique was highlighted by his suit. He smiled. "Stephanie, aren't you going to introduce me?"

Stephanie looked like she'd rather eat dirt, but instead she reluctantly turned to Eli. "Eli Goldstein, this is Joe Harrison, my...a friend of the family." She turned to Joe. "This is Eli Goldstein."

Joe extended his hand to shake just as Lucky lunged. Only Joe's quick reflexes prevented him from pouncing on Eli.

Whether spurred by Lucky or a general dislike of lawyers who looked like male models, a current of aggression seemed to transfer to the other dogs. Aggie and Rex growled and would have also lunged if I hadn't scooped them both up.

Joe anticipated Turbo. "Platz." He gave a command in German that sounded like "Plah-tz." As a K-9 police team, Joe was well versed in Schutzhund which was used with police dog training. I knew *platz* meant down and so did Lucky and Turbo. Both dogs immediately lay down, although they stayed alert and continued to stare at Eli.

Even Steve Austin, normally, the meekest dog on the planet, seemed tense.

Eli gave another nervous chuckle. "Dogs don't like me." He shrugged and shook his head. "Especially that dog." He pointed at Lucky.

"Surprising. Dogs are usually a pretty good judge of character." Joe squatted down and gave Lucky a pat. I was standing next to him and heard him whisper, "Good boy." I was sure it wasn't a coincidence when I suddenly saw Lucky eating a hot dog that had moments ago been on Joe's plate.

"Is this Indulf?" Eli's eyes rested on Rex. "Such a little dog to be the center of so much attention."

"I've renamed him Rex," I said a bit sharply. "I named him after one of my favorite mystery authors," I explained in a softer tone.

"Oh, Rex who?"

I hesitated for a moment, taken aback. Then, I remembered my manners. Not everyone was a mystery fan. "Rex Stout. He wrote the Nero Wolfe Detective Series."

There was still no light of recognition in his eyes, but he flashed a smile, which failed to weaken my knees.

Dixie came back outside and joined the group.

"Mary and Fergus Kilpatrick are really anxious about this little guy." He reached over to pet the poodle.

Rex nipped at his fingers.

Eli quickly withdrew his hand.

I was so shocked, I merely stared for several seconds. Aggie growled and Rex added to the confusion with a high-pitched yap. I didn't want to ignite the other dogs and gave both dogs a firm. "No."

There was a rumble from all of the dogs, but between Joe and Dixie, they managed to get them all under control.

Red finished his call and rejoined the group.

Eli gave an arrogant smile. "All of the male dogs must all be jealous." He placed an arm around Stephanie's waist.

A red flush rose up Stephanie's neck.

Dixie, Red and Joe stared at Eli with a wary look.

I laughed to break the tension. "Eli, you remember Red? He's the TBI officer that is investigating the murder."

"Oh yes." He laughed nervously and looked around. "You aren't still investigating?"

"Law enforcement officers are always on duty." He paused, but then added, "However, this is just dinner with my good friends."

Dixie scooted back and I could tell she was preparing to leave. However, I managed to catch her attention and used my eyes to plead with her to stay. Fortunately, after twenty-five years, she recognized that I wasn't having a stroke and sat back in her chair.

I breathed a sigh of relief and took a long swallow of my pop. For a few seconds, I wished I was drinking something stronger than Diet Coke.

"I don't want to interrupt." Eli flashed his super big smile again.

For a few moments, the awkwardness continued. Then, I remembered my manners. "Eli, please have a seat. Would you like a beer?"

He sat down. "Sure, do you have a Newcastle Brown Ale?"

I looked across at Red who shook his head and pulled out a common beer which he and Joe were drinking. "I'm sorry, but I don't think we have that brand." I started to rise. "Would you prefer wine instead?"

He waved me down. "No, please don't get up. I'm sure this will be just fine." He took the bottle Red handed him. Wiping his hands on his pants, he then looked around. "Do you have a bottle opener?"

Red took the beer and titled the bottle against the table and with one quick thrust, popped the cap and handed back the beer.

"Thank you." Eli took a sip. From the expression on his face, it was clear he didn't like the beer, but he smiled and put the bottle down on the table. "Wow. That's something." He coughed. "I usually drink ales. Once, when I was travelling with Mr. Lowry, he managed to get his hands on a couple of bottles of Antarctic Nail Ale when we were in Europe and… man was that something."

Red stared at him. "Isn't that the Australian ale which is made from an iceberg they fly in from Antarctica?"

Eli nodded excitedly. "Yes. I'm surprised you've heard of it."

Red's eyes flashed for a moment and the nerve alongside his jaw throbbed. He narrowed his eyes. "Why?"

Eli was taken aback by the blunt question and the smile froze on his face. "Excuse me? Why, what?"

"Why are you surprised that I would have heard of it?" His voice dripped icicles.

Dixie mumbled, "Danger. Danger Will Robinson."

Eli was probably too young to get the reference.

I tried to use mental telepathy to get Red to take it easy, but he wasn't making eye contact with me. Instead, he had flipped the switch which turned him into a cop, and like a Canadian Mountie he was determined to get his man.

The air was charged and short of pouring the beer in Red's lap, I couldn't think of any way to stop him.

After a few moments, Eli gave a nervous laugh. "Well, it's rather expensive and not a lot of people know of it."

Red glared and leaned forward. He opened his mouth to speak, but I interrupted. "I'm not much of a beer drinker myself." I held up my Diet Coke. An idea flashed through my head. "Eli, you're from the South, right?"

He nodded.

"What do you call this?" I held up my can of Diet Coke.

He looked at me as though he expected a trap. "Diet Coke?"

I sighed. "We were talking about the different word choices in various regions. I'm originally from Indiana and I call this a pop, but Dixie and Red are from the south and they call it *soda pop.*"

He tore his gaze away from Rex and nodded. "I get it." He glanced over at Rex again. "It's obvious, you're very attached to…Rex. However, as Executor for Archibald Lowry's will, I think he would consider the dog as part of the estate, which technically conveys to the Kilpatricks." He extended his hands. "However, the Kilpatricks are reasonable people and have made a very generous offer for the dog…given your attachment. I think we could avoid a lengthy drawn out court proceeding—"

In a flash, both Joe and Red were no longer regular citizens enjoying a leisurely dinner with friends. They were law enforcement officers. The air crackled with an electric charge. Red leaned forward. "That dog belongs to Lilly. I'd advise you and the Kilpatricks to remember that. Until a judge orders her to surrender the dog, it belongs to her." He glared.

There was another awkward silence until eventually Eli stood up. "I should probably be going."

Stephanie stood too. "I'll see you to the door."

After a brief delay, Red stood and extended his hand to shake hands with Eli. Despite the gesture, there was an authoritative air about him which screamed *law enforcement. Don't mess with me!*

Joe stood too and with that same air of authority, shook hands with Eli.

Eli turned to go, but Joe stopped him and once again extended a hand, but this time rather than shaking, he pulled a long red hair from Eli's shoulder.

Eli laughed. "It's a wonder I'm not completely covered in hair with all of these dogs." He extended his hand toward the five dogs. The two poodles who were curled up on my lap, stared. Lucky and Turbo were still lying by Joe's side but hadn't stopped staring at Eli. Steve Austin, Red's adopted dog was sitting with his nose in Red's lap.

Dixie rose. "I've got to get home too."

I started toward the door to see Dixie out, but was afraid to leave for fear of a double homicide. Red looked like he wanted to shoot Eli and Stephanie looked as though she would like nothing better than to throttle Joe.

Dixie must have sensed my dilemma. "You don't have to see me out."

I sighed. "We'll see you tomorrow at dog class."

Dixie stopped. "You'll see me tomorrow afternoon at Morrison Middle School in Cleveland. Did you forget? We've got that demonstration."

"I did forget." I looked cautiously at my friend. "Is it atop a mountain?"

"No, it's straight up 75-North and completely flat." She chuckled. "I can send you directions tomorrow. Unless you want me to pick you up?"

I shook my head. "As long as I don't have to drive Mount Everest, I'll be fine, unless you want to drive?"

"I'll be by to pick you up around noon." She smiled and left.

Stephanie showed Eli out. When I knew they were out of earshot, I stood. "Red, could I talk to you in private for a moment, please?"

He stood up. Before he left, he turned to Joe. "If I'm not back in thirty minutes, call for back up."

Joe smiled. "I got your six."

I handed Red one of the poodles and walked inside. He followed me to the bedroom. I opened the door and waited for him to enter before closing the door after me.

He smirked. "Well, maybe I won't need backup after all." He leaned forward to kiss me, but I sidestepped him.

"Red, will you be serious?" I glared. "I appreciate you sticking up for me, but don't you think you were a bit...harsh with Eli?"

He sighed. "Sorry, there's just something about that guy I don't like." He shook his head. "He's too...pretty."

I worked to keep from laughing. "He can't help the way he looks."

"I know, but it's not just that...He looks like a model. He doesn't like dogs." He held up Rex. "He wants to take your dog. He's coming between Joe and Stephanie and...I don't like his hair."

This time I couldn't stop myself and I laughed. "Will you be serious?"

"I am serious."

I stared. "And, how did Joe just happen to come down for a visit at the same time that Stephanie is here?"

He squirmed. "Joe and I were talking, and I mentioned I was working a double homicide and then I mentioned about someone trying to steal your dog. I didn't invite him to come, but..." He looked sheepish. "I also didn't tell him not to come." He paced. "If I was in his place, I'd probably do the same thing."

"I'm not upset that Joe's here."

He paused. "You're not?"

"Of course not." I smiled. "Stephanie might have another opinion entirely, but I like Joe."

He took a deep breath. "Then, why am I in trouble?"

"Who said you were in trouble?"

He looked perplexed.

"Stephanie and Joe are going to need a little time and I suspect a little privacy."

That's when we heard raised voices. We couldn't hear exact words, but there was definitely a lot of heat behind them. After a few minutes, I heard a door slam, marching and then the door to the guest room slammed. After a brief pause, there was another door slam and then the front door slammed. In a few moments, I heard the slam of a car door.

Red handed me Rex, leaned down and gave me a kiss. He paused for a moment and looked into my eyes. "Promise me, you'll be careful."

I nodded. I had every intention of keeping that promise.

Chapter 14

He walked out and I heard the sound of a truck starting and driving away.

Stephanie didn't leave her room for the remainder of the night. When I woke up the next morning, I found her sitting outside on the back deck drinking coffee with Lucky beside her chair.

I opened the door and let out Aggie and Rex. "Do you want company?" She shook her head.

I went back inside. Despite the fact that Linda Kay said I could take time off or work from home, there were still a few things I wanted to clear up in the office. So, I showered, dressed and prepared to go to the office.

I stepped back outside. Stephanie hadn't moved. "I need to go into the office for a couple of hours. If you want the car, I can—"

"I don't need it. I'm not going anywhere."

As a mother, there was a part of me that wanted to sit down and talk to my daughter and make everything better. There was another part of me that has learned from experience that when it comes to matters of the heart, the best plan is to sit back and wait until she was ready to talk.

"Okay, dear. I'll be back in a couple of hours." I paused but got no response. "Call if you need anything."

She nodded.

I hesitated a few seconds, but finally turned and walked out.

Preparing for an audit can be a nerve-wracking experience, no matter how fastidious your accounting methods. However, this audit was my first since I'd been hired by the museum to clean up the mess the previous accountant, and I use the term *accountant* lightly, created. I cleaned up the mess and worked with the IRS to resolve the problems caused when someone who doesn't know the slightest thing about accounting is hired because he's a descendent of the founders rather than for his accounting knowledge. I knew the museum's books were in good shape, but I was still nervous and wanted to make sure every *i* was dotted and every *t* was crossed.

After a couple of hours, I headed home. I wasn't surprised to find Dixie's RV in my driveway. When I went inside and didn't find anyone, I knew she and Stephanie must be out on the back deck. I hurried to my bedroom and changed into a comfortable pair of blue jeans and a shirt that looked presentable enough for a dog show without being too dressy. Finding appropriate clothes to wear to dog shows was becoming a challenge. I didn't want anything too nice because working at a dog show can be messy, as I learned when I spent an entire day picking up dog poop to raise money for the dog club. However, if you're competing, you wanted to look presentable because if you earned a qualification, there would undoubtedly be pictures. The last thing I wanted was to look like a street person in the unlikely event I ever managed to earn a qualification while competing with Aggie.

When I was dressed, I headed outside to the deck where Dixie and Stephanie were surrounded by four poodles and one golden.

I sat down and noticed three Styrofoam cups and a container with a dozen small bundt cakes. I leaned across the container and tried not to salivate. "Nothin' Bundt Cake?"

Dixie nodded. "Help yourself. We saved you a white chocolate raspberry."

I reached for the delicious cake which was so moist and delicious and bit down with pleasure. After a few minutes, I opened my eyes and looked at Stephanie who was smiling at me. "What?"

She shook her head. "Nothing. It's just amazing to see someone get that much enjoyment from a piece of cake."

I ignored her and took another bite. "Have you tried one?"

She nodded. "I think I've eaten three. I'm not going to fit into my clothes when I get back to Chicago."

I took a sip of the coffee from the cup Dixie slid in front of me. "Let's not talk about you going back. I want to enjoy every minute I have with you here." I glanced down at Lucky who was laying by her chair. "You and my grand-dog, Lucky." I smiled.

We sat in silence for a few moments. Eventually, Dixie broached the subject I had been reluctant to start. "Please tell me you didn't murder Joe. I like him and Turbo and could really use his help with the demo this afternoon."

"He's still alive." Stephanie hesitated. "We had words, but he was fine last night." She turned to Dixie. "You should ask him to come. I know he and Turbo love doing demos for kids. Besides, it'll keep him away from Eli."

Dixie glanced from Stephanie to me.

I shrugged.

She picked up her cell phone. "If you're sure…"

Stephanie nodded and forced a smile that didn't make it to her eyes. "Of course I'm sure, Aunt Dixie." She reached into her pocket and pulled out her cell phone. After a few swipes she rattled off Joe's number.

Dixie quickly dialed the number. After a brief conversation with Joe, she hung up and smiled. "Great. He said he'd meet us at the school."

I glanced at Stephanie. "Does that mean you won't be joining us?"

"Actually, I want to do some additional research at the law library." She glanced at me. "If that's okay with you? Of course, I can get a rental car if you're going to need—"

I shook my head. "No need for a rental."

"I'll be with Dixie at the demo and then we have obedience training tonight." I glanced at Dixie.

She nodded enthusiastically. "Your mom and I will be going to all the same places anyway, it makes sense."

The transportation issue settled, I glanced at Stephanie. "Is something bothering you?"

She frowned. "I don't know. It's just something about Archibald Lowry's will."

Dixie and I waited for her to explain.

She took a deep breath. "Archibald Lowry was a very wealthy man." She hesitated. "But it's very unusual for someone who was as wealthy as I'm told he was, to create a will that was so…well, not what I expected."

"What do you mean?"

She frowned. "Usually, someone with billions of dollars in assets would have managed their affairs better, but the will Eli showed me was…well, for lack of a better word, it was sloppy."

She looked up and our faces must have reflected that we didn't have the slightest idea what she was talking about. She took a moment to think and then started to explain.

"According to Eli, Archibald Lowry created a living trust and what's called a *pour-over will*. Sometimes people want to avoid probate which can be expensive and time consuming. So, they create a revocable living trust. Basically, the person transfers their assets into the trust to keep their loved ones from having to go through probate." She paused and glanced at us. "Are you following me?"

We both nodded.

"Good." She continued. "If the major assets have been transferred to the living trust, then when the person dies, the *pour-over will* directs whatever is left to *pour-over* into the trust and then be distributed to the beneficiaries."

I frowned. "Well, that sounds logical. What's wrong with that?"

Stephanie shook her head. "There's nothing wrong with it. It serves a lot of purposes. It's usually pretty simple because the estate plan is governed by the one document, the trust. It takes care of "leftovers"—any items the person didn't get around to transferring to the living trust before their death."

Dixie nodded. "So far, so good."

Stephanie looked from Dixie to me. "It also keeps the details of who gets what private. Trust documents, unlike a will—aren't a matter of public record after a death."

I thought for several minutes about what Stephanie said. "But you said Archibald Lowry left a will with the probate office." I frowned. "So, I'm confused."

Stephanie nodded. "Exactly. If he went to all the trouble of setting up a living trust and transferring assets to avoid naming the beneficiaries, then why deposit another will which revoked all previous wills?"

Dixie and I exchanged glances and eventually shrugged. I turned to Stephanie. "Did Eli have an explanation?"

She shook head. "He wasn't aware that Lowry had filed another will."

Dixie raised an eyebrow. "I would have thought Goldstein would have been the executor of the will. But it sounds like he didn't even know what his client was doing."

Stephanie nodded. "Exactly my point. The will Lowry filed with the probate court looked like something he found on the Internet. It had typos and the wording was awkward."

"Is it legal?" I asked.

She nodded. "It's legal, alright. But, why do it? He had a lawyer. Why not have him create a new will? Or, if he wanted to make someone else administer of the trust, then that's just a simple wording change." She stared at us. "Why did he create a completely different will and file it with the probate court, basically undoing all of the benefits of the living trust?"

We stared at each other.

"No idea." I frowned. "But inquiring minds want to know."

Chapter 15

Despite our best efforts, we weren't able to come up with an answer for why Archibald Lowry managed his funds the way he did. As tasty as the bundtinis were, we were still hungry and decided to grab lunch before we left for the demonstration. Stephanie joined us for a quick meal at a local chain, but then headed to the law library while Dixie and I headed north to the nearby town of Cleveland, Tennessee.

Cleveland was a modest sized city, with less than fifty thousand residents spread out over approximately thirty miles of land. Tennessee is an active part of the United States 'Bible Belt' and home to more than two hundred Protestant churches and one Roman Catholic church. When I was researching the general area and looking for a place to call home, I learned that Cleveland was the international headquarters of several Pentecostal religions. All of which probably explained why it was the home of my realtor and friend, Monica Jill.

Dixie drove us to Morrison Middle School, a brick structure that resembled practically every school in America. It was located near a private Christian university. Dixie explained the proximity allowed the middle school students to take advantage of the university's library and some of their faculty, making it highly desirable among Cleveland families. The front had a semi-circular driveway for parents to drop off and pick up students. However, we bypassed that and went around to a parking lot at the back of the building which was advertised for faculty members only. Dixie reached down to pull a piece of paper from her purse and stuck it in the windshield of her car. The paper gave us the right to park in the faculty lot for today only.

Behind the school was a grassy area with a track. There were dogs positioned nearby and a mob of middle schoolers petting and cuddling the animals.

Joe and Turbo were already there by the time we arrived. Joe was wearing jeans and a T-shirt, but was undoubtedly a policeman, even without the Lighthouse Dunes K-9 Division baseball cap. Turbo was wearing his vest that indicated he was working today.

Dixie walked up to Joe and gave him a big hug. "Thank you so much for agreeing to do this, especially at the last minute."

"What else do I have to do?" Joe gave a half smile. "Besides, it's keeping me from doing something stupid."

"Like what?" I asked.

"Like running a background check on Eli Goldstein."

Dixie and I exchanged glances and then we both answered together. "Do it."

He was taken aback. "What?"

"Don't let us stop you," Dixie said.

He looked at me.

"Joe, I'm Stephanie's mother and I try to stay out of her love life, but as her mother I'm also completely biased. We're in the middle of a murder investigation."

"I know, but—" He looked confused.

"Isn't it common for the police to investigate everyone in a situation like this...you know, murder?"

He half shrugged. "Yes, but I'm not assigned to the case." He rubbed the back of his neck.

"Pish posh." Dixie waved away his concerns. "I'm sure Red would love to have the help of a highly trained investigator like you." She glanced down at the Plott Hound sitting beside his partner. "And Turbo, of course."

"I'm not sure Stephanie will see it that way." He stared at us for several moments, but then I noticed the corners of his lips twitch. After a few seconds, he stopped trying to control the twitch and smiled. "Thanks."

"Mrs. Echosby," a voice called out.

I turned at the sound of my name. I looked around and saw Addison Abbott beckoning from the bleachers near the track. Next to her was Dr. Morgan.

I gave an enthusiastic wave and hurried over to the bleachers to watch my first herding exhibition.

Addison slid down and made room for me on the bleachers just as we heard Dixie's voice over an external loudspeaker.

Dixie thanked everyone for attending and the principal at Morrison Middle School for hosting the demonstration. She then gave a brief explanation of the events which would start with a herding demonstration. She introduced Mai Nguyen and her border collie, Skye. She talked a bit about the history of the breed while Mai prepared.

When she was ready, Mai gave a signal and Dixie asked the audience for silence. Mai had a trailer at the end of the field and she opened the gate, releasing four sheep. There were oohs and aahs from the crowd as the sheep pranced down the ramp and wandered around the field.

Mai had a whistle and a long wooden crook. She blew the whistle and Skye crept forward and around behind the sheep. Another blow from the whistle and Skye crouched down and waited. A long tweet and Skye continued rounding the sheep, circling closer and closer until they turned and headed in the direction she wanted. Another short blast from the whistle and she halted, changed course and herded the sheep in the opposite direction. Mai had Skye repeat the maneuver several times.

On the loudspeaker, Dixie whispered like an announcer at a golf tournament and explained that herding dogs like border collies were used in farming to help bring sheep down from one pasture to the next or with lambing.

Mai gave three blasts from her whistle and Skye took off toward the sheep. The startled animals started to run and Skye chased and prodded them in the direction she wanted, all without touching them. Skye singled one of the sheep away from the others and was pushing it toward a small makeshift pen which was placed at one corner of the field. Eventually at a blast from Mai's whistle, Skye coaxed the sheep into the pen which was quickly closed.

The crowded applauded.

Dixie explained how a herding dog was invaluable for ranchers and farmers during lambing season.

Mai blew her whistle again and Skye led the remainder of the sheep into the pen.

At the end of the demonstration, Dixie cautioned the crowd to do extensive research before purchasing a dog. "Border Collies are excellent herding dogs, but these dogs need a job. They are highly intelligent and were bred over centuries to herd. A border collie will herd ducks, sheep, cattle, children or cars." The crowd laughed. "But a border collie without a job is a recipe for disaster. This is an intelligent breed which will do great on a farm, but I don't recommend them for apartments."

At the end of the demonstration, Addison clapped enthusiastically. "That was amazing. I wish we had a farm and I could get a border collie."

Dr. Morgan smiled. "Farms are a lot of work."

"I know, but if we had a farm, I could practice being a vet with all of the different animals."

Dr. Morgan stood. "I'm going to see if Mai needs help getting the sheep back in the trailer." Next, Dixie introduced Joe and Turbo. Both were accustomed to doing demonstrations for children in Lighthouse Dunes. Dixie gave Joe the microphone and he explained that Turbo was a Plott Hound.

"Anyone ever heard of a Plott Hound?" he asked.

There were a few hands.

"They aren't well-known, but they are one of the few hounds which originated in the United States. These dogs were bred to track bear and wild boar."

There was an appreciative rumble from the crowd.

"Needless to say, these dogs are fearless. They are excellent in search and rescue and as a police dog, they are also great with what we call bite work." Joe gave Turbo a few commands in German which Turbo followed to the letter.

While he talked, Dixie slipped beside me and tapped Addison on the shoulder beckoning for her to follow. The two slipped behind a trailer. After a few moments, Dixie returned alone carrying Addison's sweater.

When Joe was near the end of the demonstration, Dixie walked up and handed him the sweater then took the microphone. She explained that Turbo was going to search for a lost girl. She cautioned everyone to remain still while the dog tracked.

Joe placed the sweater in front of Turbo and let the dog sniff, then he took the leash and gave the dog the command to find. Turbo put his nose to the ground and walked around the grounds. When he got to the bleachers, he sniffed the seat where Addison had sat earlier, but then continued to follow the path that she and Dixie had taken. When he got to the trailer, he sat down. Addison stood up and showed the crowd that he had, indeed, tracked and found his prey. The crowd applauded. Joe returned Addison's sweater and she returned to the bleachers.

Dixie then demonstrated obedience commands with Chyna and Leia. Aggie and Rex were there purely for petting. However, after months of attending similar functions with Dixie, I was able to tell the small crowd of people who came to pet the dogs basic facts about poodles. I was amazed how much I'd learned about the breed in a short period of time, and relayed how the breed was also highly intelligent, easy to train and don't shed.

When the event was over, the school thanked Dixie and all of the exhibitors. Then they gave us the greatest gift of all: the football team's assistance in putting away all of our equipment, which cut down clean up time to a fraction of what it normally took.

It wasn't until Dixie and I loaded the four poodles into the RV and sat down that I realized how tired I was—tired and hungry. My stomach growled so loudly Rex, who was sitting on my lap, jumped down. We laughed.

"I guess we better get you something to eat," Dixie joked.

The principal agreed to watch the trailer and the sheep so we could grab a quick bite before we headed back to Chattanooga. So, Mai left her truck and rode with Dr. Morgan to a seafood restaurant located in the downtown area.

Downtown Cleveland, Tennessee was a quaint area with cobblestoned, tree lined streets, brick store fronts, and colonial and Victorian houses. The restaurant was small and situated near the town's one and only art museum.

Joe removed Turbo's vest and left him in the air-conditioned RV with the other dogs while we ate.

It was clear that Dr. Morgan was very fond of Mai. Surprisingly, the beautiful gamekeeper seemed equally fond of the coroner, if their playful banter was anything to go by.

After we placed our orders, Dr. Morgan mentioned that he was going to help Mai take the sheep back up the mountain and wouldn't make obedience class tonight.

He glanced at Joe several times out of the corner of his eyes, clearly unsure if he could be trusted.

Dixie patted his hand. "If you have something to say, you can speak freely."

Dr. Morgan nodded. "I completed the autopsy on Archibald Lowry." He followed up with a lot of technical jargon that I think amounted to the fact that cause of death was due to the stab wound he received. Which wasn't surprising. What came next was. "However, I took the liberty of running a few additional toxicology screens." He took a deep breath. "More than I would normally have done, but based on some information I received." He colored and avoided looking directly at Mai.

She rolled her eyes and patted his hand. "It's okay. I don't mind saying that I thought Archibald Lowry had been acting strangely the last few weeks." She shrugged. "Well, he was always strange, but the past few weeks he was even *more* strange."

Joe leaned forward. "You found something in the toxicology report?"

Dr. Morgan nodded. "Arsenic. Archibald Lowry was being poisoned."

Chapter 16

After a few seconds, the shock wore off.

Dixie leaned forward. "What? Who? How?"

I added, "Why?"

Dr. Morgan held up a hand to fend off the questions. "Arsenic is tasteless and odorless. Hair, toenails and fingernails tend to hold the poison and are great for testing."

Mai leaned over. "Isn't arsenic pretty much everywhere? I mean isn't it in rat poison? Plus, it's also in the food and water."

"Yes and no. It's not actually used in rat poison anymore. However, you're right that it's a lot more common than most people think. It's in our food and water in extremely low doses. It was also used in paint dyes and wallpaper."

"But wouldn't he have shown signs of being sick?" I asked.

Dr. Morgan shrugged. "It probably would have seemed like gastrointestinal problems."

We were so engrossed in our discussion of arsenic that we completely forgot about our food. When the server arrived with our plates, we were all a bit hesitant to begin eating.

After a moment of hesitation, we laughed and shook off the creepy arsenic fog that had descended over our table.

We set aside discussions of arsenic and poison while we ate and enjoyed friendly conversation. Afterward, Dr. Morgan and Mai left to go get the sheep and make the long trek up the mountain.

Joe walked back to the RV where he found Turbo asleep and surrounded by poodles. Joe smiled, shook his head and then gave a whistle which caused the dog to bound toward him like a rocket. The two left and headed back to Chattanooga.

Dixie and I let the poodles take care of their business and then we headed for the dog club.

The East Tennessee Dog Club was a long, low building with a metal roof. It wasn't fancy, but it was located on over three acres of land which was mostly fenced and provided a great venue for dog shows. The building also offered tons of parking, another must have for dog shows and training facilities.

When we pulled up to the building, the poodles immediately stood and started their stretches.

B.J. and Monica Jill were inside getting in a few minutes of last-minute practice before class.

Without Dr. Morgan and his German shepherd, Max, class went relatively quickly but lacked a certain something which I couldn't put my finger on. Nevertheless, we all put our best foot forward as we worked on heeling with our dogs on leash. Dixie brought out several telephone books. Then she took her standard poodle Chyna and demonstrated what she wanted us to do.

"First, let me demonstrate heeling off leash for you." She stood very still with Chyna on her left. "The dog is always on your left side and you can have your hand by your leg or across your stomach. I recommend your stomach." She placed her arm across her stomach, looked down and said, "Chyna heel."

Chyna walked beside Dixie and appeared to be glued to her leg. She was careful not to get too far in front or behind Dixie and her eyes never left Dixie's face.

Dixie said, "Fast." Then she trotted and Chyna picked up her pace to keep up. "Slow." She slowed her pace and the dog adjusted. "Normal." She maintained a normal pace. When she got close to the wall, she said, "Left turn." Chyna practically pivoted in place to execute the left-hand turn, but she did it without leaving Dixie's side. Dixie executed a right turn, an about turn and finally halted. When they were done, she said, "Finish." She did a flourish with the arm on her stomach and Chyna did a small jump, kicked her butt into place and sat. Chyna didn't move until Dixie said, "Free." Then she received a lot of praise and a jackpot from the bait bag Dixie wore around her waist. "Good girl."

We applauded. We'd seen Dixie demonstrate heeling with Chyna and Leia before and it was always a thing of beauty.

"Tonight we're going to work on the pivot which will be helpful for the turns and for finishes."

Dixie handed each of us a telephone book which we placed on the floor. Standing next to the book, the first challenge was getting our dogs to place both front feet on it. Initially, we gave a treat for one paw. Then we only treated for two paws. I was proud to see Aggie seemed to pick up what I was asking her to do the quickest. On the opposite extreme was Jac who thought the telephone book was a toy. When Monica Jill moved beside him, he grabbed the book in his mouth and took off. A game of chase ensued until Dixie told Monica Jill not to play and suggested she sit down and wait. When Jac saw his owner wasn't going to pursue him, he ripped the telephone book to shreds. When he was done with his fun, he returned to his owner who sat with her head in her hands.

Snoball, the West Highland Terrier, was terrified of the telephone book and took a lot of coaxing to put even one paw on the book. By the time she finally got a paw on the book, Dixie told B.J. to give her a treat and then stop. "No point in getting her stressed out."

B.J. wiped sweat from her forehead. "Stress her out? I'm sweating like a hooker at a Baptist revival."

Monica Jill was still avoiding making eye contact with Jac who was doing his best to shove his ball in her hands.

Dixie patted her on the shoulder. "Look, this isn't easy for dogs. He doesn't know what you want, yet."

"I'm pretty sure he knows I didn't want that telephone book shredded."

Dixie chuckled. "Really? I'm not so sure. Look at him." She waited until Monica Jill lifted her head. "He thinks he just saved your life from that scary book."

Jac stared so lovingly at Monica Jill that she eventually shook her head and gave her dog a hug.

"Remember, he's still a puppy and has a lot of energy. Have you found another place to take him for doggie daycare?"

Monica Jill shook her head. "I've been meaning to find another place, since Pet Haven closed. I've been struggling to find another place I liked as much."

"I'll give you the names of a couple of places you can try, but he really needs to get rid of some of his energy."

"Actually, I was thinking about hiring Addison to help him burn off some energy. She's great with dogs. She runs track and would be able to run with him and, hopefully, tire him out on the weekends and when school is out during the summer."

Dixie smiled. "I think that's an excellent idea." She glanced over at me. "I talked to Mai a little today and she might be another good resource. Now that Archibald Lowry's dead, she's looking for another position. A doggie daycare with boarding might be just the place."

Monica Jill perked up. "That would be great."

Dixie smiled down at Jac. "He's a great dog and he just wants to please you."

Monica Jill sighed. "Thank you for reminding me." She patted her dog and then picked up his ball and tossed it across the room.

Jac sped off to get the ball and bring it back.

We let all of the dogs, except Rex, go outside into the fenced area to play while we cleaned up the room. Rex was just a puppy and I was afraid he'd get trampled. When we were done, we sat down outside and watched the dogs. I let Rex play with the other dogs while I could keep an eye on him. However, I needn't have worried. Aggie was a good big sister and gave Jac a nip when he ran too fast and barreled into Rex. He didn't make that mistake again.

While we sat and watched our dogs, Dixie and I shared the information we'd learned from both Red and Dr. Morgan. When B.J. and Monica Jill heard about Archibald Lowry's will, they were dumbstruck. Monica Jill recovered first.

"That's wonderful, Dixie. Just think of all the poodles you'll be able to save with half a billion dollars."

Dixie shook her head. "I'm not going to count my poodles before they're rescued. A lot can happen, and I have a feeling Archibald Lowry's relatives will have something to say about that will."

B.J. nodded. "You got that right. Those two were definitely expecting to inherit their cousin's money. They'll contest the will and keep that money tied up until you're too old or too broke to fight anymore."

"Can they do that?" Monica Jill asked.

"I can ask Stephanie tonight, but I'm pretty sure they can."

B.J. smiled. "How are Stephanie and that handsome hunk?"

"I have no idea." I watched to make sure Rex was okay and then continued, "Honestly, I know he's handsome and—"

"And he's a lawyer, so he should have plenty of money," B.J. added.

Monica Jill tiled her head. "She doesn't need his money. She's a lawyer herself. I'm sure she has plenty of money."

B.J. gave Monica Jill a *you poor pitiful fool* look, "Honey, you can never have too much money."

Monica Jill returned the look. "Now, you know there are more important things in a relationship than money. Don't pretend you're that mercenary."

"You got me." B.J. laughed. "There *are* more important things than money in a relationship. However, money definitely helps. Besides, that Eli is nice eye candy."

"He's very handsome, but that policeman was handsome too," Monica Jill added.

"Hmm. Yes, he was." B.J. nodded. "What ever happened to him?"

I gave a brief outline of his surprise visit.

"That's so romantic," Monica Jill said.

"As much as I like to look at Eli, you tell Stephanie she should go with the policeman. He sounds like the kind of man who'll be around for the tough times as well as the good times." B.J. gave me a serious look. "Besides, I don't trust a man that don't like dogs."

"I never trust a man that doesn't like dogs." Dixie smiled. "But I always trust a dog who doesn't like a man."

"Amen, sister," Monica Jill said.

We talked about Joe and Eli and I was pleased that the group all seemed to be pulling for Joe. When we'd exhausted conversation on my daughter's love life, we returned to the matter at hand.

"Well, I called Fiona Darling and hired her to investigate a few claims I have...excuse me." B.J. got up and went to clean up after Snoball. When she returned, she asked, "Where was I?"

"You hired Fiona Darling," Dixie reminded her.

"I asked for references first, of course, and called her last employer."

I frowned. "I thought she was self-employed."

B.J. nodded. "She is, now, but she used to work for NKC Holdings and Trust."

I frowned. "What's NKC?"

"Norman, King and Croy. It's one of the biggest insurance companies in the world. They're almost as big as Lloyd's of London."

"Why'd she leave?" I asked.

"Well, officially they aren't supposed to share anything except the years she worked, but I talked to this really nice man who told me that she was fired." She gave us a knowing stare.

Monica Jill leaned forward. "Why'd they fire her?"

"He said she was obsessed with a case." B.J. paused for a moment. "Do y'all remember that bank robbery that happened about...oh, it must have been twenty years ago now. One of the bank tellers was murdered. The police got one of the men, but the money was never recovered."

A light bulb flashed in my head. "Wait, I think that's the bank that Ivan Bradington, the butler, served time for."

She nodded and pulled up her cell phone. "I looked it up after I talked to Timmy."

"Timmy?" Monica Jill asked.

B.J. nodded. "He was my contact." She scrolled on her phone until she found the item. "Yes, Ivan Bradington served twenty years for the murder of a bank teller. There were two other men, but they got away."

"Well, well. So, Fiona Darling was investigating the robbery that Ivan Bradington committed. Coincidence?" I stared at Dixie. "I think not."

The only other information we learned was that Archibald Lowry was planning to sell his estate. Monica Jill was playing telephone tag with the listing agent but hoped to get more information before we met again on Thursday.

Finished with our updates, we called for our dogs, locked up the building and left. Just as Dixie was pulling out of the parking lot, I got a call on my cell phone. I didn't recognize the number but answered anyway.

"Hello."

"Is this Mrs. Echosby?"

When I recognized Mrs. Huntington's voice, I took a deep breath. "Yes, hello Mrs. Huntington. I've been meaning to call you, but—"

"Listen, I don't have much time." She paused for a brief moment and then hurried on. "Were you able to talk to your friend about a position?"

I put the phone on speaker and took a deep breath. "Yes, I did, however I'm afraid we won't be able to help."

"I'm a good cook and housekeeper. I've always managed to give satisfactory service." She hurried on with a panicked edge to her voice. "Maybe, they'd be willing to try a trial period. I'm sure given a chance I can—"

Hearing the desperation in her voice was hard, but I decided to rip the bandage off and get it over with. "Mrs. Huntington, I'm sure you're an excellent cook and housekeeper, it's just that…well, we have concerns that you have a drinking problem and—"

"Ahhh, that's it, well I ain't denying that I had a problem, but I've paid…I'm still paying. Every time I close my eyes. I know what I've done and I see it, every night." There was a catch in her voice. "I ain't had a drop of liquor in over twenty-years. Not since…well, as God is my witness, I ain't had a drink since… I'm a desperate woman." She sobbed. "I can't stay here. It's just not safe."

"What do you mean? Mrs. Huntington, what's going on?" I asked.

Mrs. Huntington whispered. "I can't talk now. I just need to go."

Dixie exchanged a glance with me and then said. "Mrs. Huntington, this is Dixie Jefferson, Lilly's friend. You can come and work for me. We can pick you up first thing tomorrow."

"Tomorrow will be too late." She whispered, "Oh no, did you hear something?"

"Mrs. Huntington, maybe you should call the police."

The line went dead.

"Mrs. Huntington…" I yelled into the cell phone as though the increased volume would generate a response.

I looked at Dixie as she bypassed the exit which would take me to my house and headed up Signal Mountain. I dialed Red and prayed we'd make it in time.

Chapter 17

"Red, I just got a weird call from Mrs. Huntington. I think she's in danger."

"Did you call 9-1-1?"

"No, I called you."

"What do you mean by weird?"

I quickly explained what happened.

"It could be that her phone lost power. Did you try calling her back?"

His logic was getting on my nerves, especially since he could very well be right. I took a deep breath. "Listen, I can't explain it, but that woman was terrified. Dixie and I are on our way and—"

"What? No, leave this to the professionals. If there is something wrong, they'll handle it."

"The professionals don't believe there's a problem."

He was silent for several moments. "Point taken." He sighed. "I'll call the police and ask them to stop by the house, but if there is a problem, there's nothing that you and Dixie can do except make matters worse and possibly get yourselves killed." I heard rustling and then a door close. "Joe and I are on our way, but I need you and Dixie to go home and wait."

In the background I heard dogs barking and the sound of a car door slam. Joe asked a question which I didn't hear and then Red asked, "Is Stephanie with you?"

"No."

He relayed the message and then I heard the sound of his truck starting. "I'm going to hang up and call 9-1-1. Will you and Dixie please STAND DOWN. We'll take it from here."

I glanced at Dixie who had pulled the RV over. She nodded. "Okay, but call me and let me know what happened."

He gave me his word and hung up.

It was too dark for Dixie to see my face, so she must have sensed the anguish in my voice. "He's right you know. There's not really anything we can do. We need to leave it to the professionals." She reached across the seat and squeezed my hand. "Although, we do have four poodles and I'm sure Beau has a Glock in the glovebox." She gave me a mischievous grin. "We can storm the place like Thelma and Louise on steroids."

I smiled. "Maybe not. Things didn't end so well for them."

"Good point."

I couldn't help but stare at the glovebox after that. I knew Dixie was an excellent shot and both she and Beau carried concealed weapons. In fact, practically everyone I knew in Chattanooga carried a weapon except me. I glanced at my friend. "Aren't you afraid you'll hurt someone with that gun?"

Dixie chuckled. "That's the intent."

"You know what I mean."

She laughed. "I've been around guns my entire life so I'm comfortable with them. Besides, I had to go through a lot of classes to get my concealed carry permit." She sighed. "Now, that Glock isn't my favorite gun. I prefer my little Smith and Wesson. The Glock is light-weight and the safety is different. I have to manually take the safety off of my revolver, but the Glock you just have to squeeze the trigger."

"That sounds dangerous."

"My daddy always said, you don't squeeze that trigger unless you want to shoot someone. If you want to shoot someone, then you better squeeze that trigger."

I shivered at the thought. My husband, Albert, used to have a gun, but I was never comfortable with them. I forced myself to focus on something other than the glovebox.

Dixie found a driveway where she turned around the RV and we headed back down the mountain.

When I got home, I was happy to see the lights on and I knew Stephanie was safe. It was late and Dixie wasn't staying, so I took the poodles inside after promising to text her as soon as I heard from Red.

Stephanie and Lucky were pacing the floor. When we entered, she flew at me. "What on earth have you been up to?"

I was taken aback. "We went to the dog demonstration and then dog club."

"Why is Joe insisting that I send him a text the moment you get home?" She pulled up her cell phone and punched a few letters.

"It's a long story. I'm going to need some wine. Why don't you pour us both glasses while I let the dogs out?"

Stephanie took a bottle of Moscato from the wine rack and waited for me on the sofa while I let all three of the dogs out back.

When they were done, I let them back inside and gave each of them treats which I knew would keep them occupied while Stephanie and I talked.

It didn't take long to tell her about Mrs. Huntington, although glancing at my cell phone every thirty seconds didn't make it ring any faster. I filled in the time by updating her on what we'd learned from Dr. Morgan, B.J. and Monica Jill. By the time I finished, my phone rang and Stephanie's dinged indicating she had a text message.

Red sounded tired and out of breath. "Mrs. Huntington took a tumble down a flight of stairs." I started to interrupt, but he continued on. "She's being rushed to the hospital." He paused and even though I couldn't see him, I knew he was rubbing the back of his neck. "She hit her head and we're not sure about the extent of her other injuries, but she's alive... thanks to you."

I released the breath I'd been holding ever since I picked up the phone. "Do you know what happened? How did she fall?"

"We're working on it, but it appears she'd been drinking and slipped. It looks like it was an accident."

"But that's not possible. I mean, she said she hasn't had a drink in over twenty years."

Red was silent for several moments. "Lilly, I'm sorry, but her breath smelled of alcohol and we found a flask in her pocket."

I was shocked. "She lied to me."

"Looks that way."

We spoke for a few additional moments, and then he promised to fill me in later.

Stephanie looked at me anxiously. "I need details. Joe just said she's alive." She refilled her glass from the bottle and topped off mine. "Men can be so frustrating."

I smiled. "Well, I'm sure Joe was just trying to be mindful of your feelings. After all, you two aren't really a couple at the moment."

She sipped her wine and gave Lucky, who was sitting nearby with his head on her lap, a scratch. "You're the exception, aren't you boy?"

He wagged his tail and looked at her with his big brown eyes.

I filled her in on what Red had told me and sent Dixie a text message. She had just arrived home and said we'd make a trip to the hospital tomorrow to check on Mrs. Huntington.

Stephanie and I talked about Mrs. Huntington for several more minutes however, until I noticed she had a frown and seemed distracted.

"What's wrong? Did you find what you were looking for at the law library?"

She nodded. "Pretty much. The will Archibald Lowry presented at probate is legal and supersedes all previous wills." She shrugged. "I knew that, but I was trying to find information on the trust and that was harder to find." She paused. "Mom, do you think Madison could find out the state of Archibald Lowry's finances?"

I shrugged. "I'm sure she could. According to Red, she's an excellent hacker and now that she works for the TBI, she can do it legally." I looked at my daughter. "It is legal isn't it?"

"That depends on who you talk to." She laughed. "Red should definitely be able to access the bank statements, but I'm not sure about the trust. He'd probably have to access the trust administrator, which would be Eli."

I looked carefully at Stephanie. "Do you think he would grant it?"

She frowned. "I'm not sure, but…" She smiled. "I'm sure Red can be very convincing when he wants to be."

"He is, but…he's also a softie deep down inside." I tucked my legs under me, cupped my wineglass and smiled.

Stephanie stared at me with a large grin on her face. "You're really happy aren't you?"

I thought for a moment. "Yes, I am." I glanced around. "This house isn't much and I'm only renting for now, but—"

"Oh, I almost forgot." Stephanie hopped up from the sofa and hurried back into the guest room. After a few moments, she came back and handed me a large manila envelope.

I opened the envelope and read the papers inside.

"I got the person who's been using Dad's identity." She leaned over and pointed to one of the sheets. "Actually, I couldn't have done it without Madison's help."

I glanced at her. "Madison?"

"She was able to track the IP addresses or some other techie stuff… anyway, bottom line is she tracked down the person and I got the police to arrest them. They found all kinds of stuff including credit cards, social security information and tons of stuff on over thirty people he was stealing from. Joe helped me work with the police in Arizona to get him extradited." She gazed down and spoke very softly. "Joe even volunteered to go and bring him to Lighthouse Dunes so we could charge him."

"He's a good man."

She nodded. "I know."

I smiled. "My friend from the dog club, B.J., thinks he's hot too."

She grinned. "Well, he isn't as handsome as Eli, but...he's definitely got his good qualities." She sighed. "Eli is very handsome. He gets a lot of looks from women and some of them practically throw themselves at him." She sat back on the sofa and stared down into her glass. "Tonight, while we were at dinner, some redheaded amazon cornered him on his way to the restroom. She was all over him and then later, some woman actually bought him a drink and sent the waitress over with her phone number." She stared at me. "Can you believe it?"

"Wow, that's bold." I took a deep breath and tentatively asked, "Did he send back the drink?"

"No." She shook her head. "Can you believe it? I told him he should, but he didn't. He drank it." She sighed. "He said I was making too much of a slight gesture and it would be rude to send the drink back.

"I tried to find a polite way to say it seemed rude *not* to send it back but couldn't find the right words." She petted Lucky. "It's not like we're a couple, but...it made me feel...oh, I don't know. It made me feel like, if he couldn't even see why accepting a drink from another woman while he's out on a date with me was a problem then...we probably didn't share the same views on what monogamy means."

"Well, maybe he's a lot more sensitive than he comes across and really didn't want to hurt the woman's feelings."

I don't think I fooled Stephanie based on the look she gave me. After a few moments, she shrugged. "It's not like I want to marry him, but it would be nice if he acted like I was...oh, I don't know...special, like J—"

"You are special, and I hope you find someone who makes you feel like you are."

She sighed. "We're going to dinner again tomorrow too, so we'll see."

"Yes, we'll see."

We talked a bit longer and then went to bed. When I woke up, I had a text message from Linda Kay.

Stay home. Enjoy time with your daughter.

I responded with a *thanks*. Stephanie was going to the law library again today and then dinner later with Eli, but maybe we could go out for breakfast if I hurried.

I rolled out of bed and grabbed the poodles then headed down the hall to let them outside. As I passed the guest room, I tapped lightly on the door.

"Come in."

I opened the door and stuck my head inside. "I hope I didn't wake you."

Stephanie yawned. "No, I'm awake."

"How about breakfast?"

"Pancakes?"

"Sounds good."

Lucky stretched.

"Lucky, come."

He turned to look at Stephanie, who gave him the okay, before he followed me. I opened the back door and waited to make sure that all three dogs took care of all of the calls of nature before letting them back inside.

Stephanie and I got dressed and went to a local restaurant I discovered which was well known for fresh food and great coffee. Afterward, we spent a little time shopping. The silent auction was in a few days and Stephanie hadn't packed a fancy cocktail dress. She was tall and thin and looked great in everything she tried on, so finding the perfect outfit didn't take long. In fact, she found two dresses. One was bright red, fitted with a deep plunging neckline. She looked stunning and very sexy. When the clerk entered the fitting room, Stephanie said, "I'll take it."

The sales clerk was an older woman who had pointed out several dresses which she thought not only complimented Stephanie's height and size but looked great against her skin. "That's perfect. You'll look wonderful." She held up a navy-blue dress and I heard Stephanie gasp.

She smiled. "This just came in, and I thought I'd have you take a look."

Stephanie extended a hand, went back into the dressing room and quickly came out to show me.

The dress fit as though it had been made especially for her. It was a tulle, knee-length A-line dress with a fitted bodice and a matching embroidered lace overlay. It had a high princess neck line and a simple band just above her waist.

I clasped my hands over my chest. "You look amazing," I whispered.

She gave a turn in front of the three-way mirror. "Eli will like the Red one, but...blue is Joe's favorite color."

"Which one do you like best?"

She did a twirl. "I like the blue. It feels like it was made for me."

I nodded.

She took one last look in the mirror, turned and headed to the dressing room. "I'll take them both."

I bought a simple black dress which I could wear to work, but planned to wear tonight to dinner with Red. I considered another dress which the sales clerk thought would look good on me too. It was a navy-blue sheath dress with what she called a 'cold shoulder' design, which basically meant the shoulders were cut out. It showcased more of my body than I normally felt comfortable with, but it looked great and I have to admit, I felt fantastic wearing it. However, one glance at the price tag had me carefully removing the dress and returning it to the clerk.

Shopping for shoes was easier. We went to a designer shoe warehouse, and Stephanie found a pair of silver peep-toe pumps on the clearance shelf which were an additional eighty percent off the clearance price. I bought two pair of work flats and a brightly colored pair of sandals which were, not eighty percent off, but were cute nonetheless.

After we finished shopping, Dixie met us for lunch and then the two of us headed to the hospital to check on Mrs. Huntington. Stephanie took our packages home and promised to let out the dogs before she headed back to the law library.

There were several hospitals in Chattanooga. I neglected to ask which hospital they took her to when I spoke to Red, but we made an educated guess and tried the one closest to Signal Mountain. When we asked at the information desk, we were rewarded with a room number and directions to get to the Intensive Care Unit. After several turns, an elevator ride and the help of two strangers, we made it to our destination. Normally Dixie and I were great with directions. The problem was our information giver neglected to specify we needed to go to the Trauma Intensive Care Unit rather than the normal intensive care.

When we walked into the room and looked at Mrs. Huntington, Dixie gasped. It was clear why she was brought here.

Her face was battered, bruised and swollen to the point that she was barely recognizable.

"She looks like someone from that movie, *The Elephant Man*," Dixie whispered.

There were tubes and wires everywhere and machines which beeped, dinged and chimed periodically.

We pulled up a chair and sat quietly. There wasn't much more we could do. While we waited, a man dressed in black with a clerical color stopped by.

"Hello, I'm Reverend Taylor. Are you members of the family?"

"No, we're just…friends. My name is Lilly Echosby and this is my friend, Dixie Jefferson."

He extended his hand and we shook.

Reverend Taylor was an older African American man with white hair, a white mustache and kind friendly face.

"Have you known Mrs. Huntington long?" He sat down in the remaining chair.

We shook our heads. "No, actually we just met her a few days ago." I couldn't believe so much had happened in such a short period of time.

"She's been unconscious since she was brought in and we weren't sure if she was a person of faith." He smiled and leaned closer. "Although, I have to admit, I'll pray for her regardless."

I smiled. "I think she was Catholic. She used to wear a crucifix and a St. Martins of Tours medallion."

He nodded. "Ah, now let me see if I remember my early training." He looked up to the right as though he was trying to find something in the back of his mind. After a few seconds, he smiled. "St. Martin is…the patron saint of…alcoholics?"

I nodded. "Very good."

He chuckled. "The sisters from Our Lady of Hungary Catholic School in South Bend, Indiana will be proud."

I stared. "You're from South Bend? I'm from Lighthouse Dunes."

He smiled bigger. "Nice to meet a fellow Hoosier. What brings you down to Chattanooga?"

I sighed. "It's a long story."

He held up a hand. "I don't mean to pry."

"No, it isn't that. It's …well, let's just say, I came looking for my 'happy place.'"

He nodded. "I like that. I hope you found it."

I nodded. "What brings you to Chattanooga?"

He stretched out his legs. "A combination of things. The weather, a desire to be closer to my grandchildren and…I guess, a call to be helpful."

"I would think ministers are helpful wherever they are," Dixie said.

He was silent for a moment. "You're right, of course, but I used to be a chaplain in the military." He gazed into space as though looking back in time. "When you're involved in life and death situations on a daily basis, it gets…well, you feel useful." He chuckled. "I guess, you could say I got bored ministering to a congregation. Christenings, baptisms, marriages and visiting the sick…well, it is important work, but…"

I smiled. "But a bit dull."

He nodded. "Here, I pray with people who are fighting life and death situations each and every day. I feel…useful."

We chatted a bit longer and then he stood up. "I've taken up enough of your time. There's a Catholic priest, Father Lee, who ministers here too. I'll let him know about Mrs. Huntington." He shook our hands and whispered, "And, I'll say a prayer for her too."

He left.

As we were leaving, we saw Mary and Fergus Kilpatrick getting off the elevator. I was in no mood to argue with Fergus about Rex, so Dixie and I hightailed it in the opposite direction. At the end of the hall, we ran into Reverend Taylor coming out of a patient's room.

He started to smile but froze when he saw me. "Is something the matter? Mrs. Huntington hasn't taken a turn for the worse already?"

I shook my head. "No, but I wonder if I could trouble you to do a favor for me."

"Of course."

"This is going to sound terrible, and I'm sorry that I can't explain it, but there are two people who are going to see Mrs. Huntington. I don't trust them. Would you make sure that they aren't left alone with her?"

Reverend Taylor gazed into my eyes for several seconds and then nodded. "I promise."

"Thank you."

He hurried down to Mrs. Huntington's room and I picked up my cell and called Red.

Chapter 18

Convincing Red that Mrs. Huntington needed security was challenging. Although that wasn't surprising considering I had no valid reason for my suspicions other than the fact that Mary and Fergus Kilpatrick creeped me out. Ultimately, he promised to 'see what he could do.'

I hung up and stared at Dixie. "Do you think we should go back? We could take turns sitting with her."

Dixie waved away my concerns with a flip of her hand as she backed out of the hospital parking lot. "No need. I'm sure Red will have someone down there shortly."

I glanced at her, wishing I had her confidence. "What makes you so certain?"

She smiled. "We're talking about the man who left his required TBI training in the wilderness in the middle of the night because you *thought* you saw a murder on a pet cam. Then he drove another two hours because, when no body was found, you got upset."

I didn't need to look in the mirror to know that I was blushing. I could feel the heat moving up my neck. "He's a good man with a kind heart."

She laughed. "Yes, he is. Plus, he happens to be crazy about you."

I grinned but quickly stopped. "You don't think I'm taking advantage of his feelings for me, do you?"

"You're not using him for your own selfish purposes. You're trying to save a woman's life." She glanced at me from the corner of her eye. "Two men are already dead, and one person is badly injured." She sighed. "Red isn't stupid nor is he a wimp. He won't do anything he doesn't want or need to do. He's also got to know that your instincts have been bang on in the past. If there's the slightest chance someone pushed Mrs. Huntington down those stairs, then he has to do whatever it takes to make sure they don't get an opportunity to finish the job."

"I wish I had some proof other than a feeling."

Dixie reached across and patted my leg. "Stop worrying about it. Give your little gray cells something else to think about and eventually the pieces will all fall into place."

Thirty minutes later, I got a text from Red stating that a policeman was on watch outside of Catherine Huntington's room. I breathed a sigh of relief. Red was a good man.

I turned to Dixie. "Do we have time to swing by the mall? There's a dress I want to pick up."

When I got home, I let the dogs outside to take care of their business. Stephanie had already left for dinner and a movie with Eli. So, I showered and dressed for dinner with Red.

When I opened the door, his reaction was more than I could have wished. He stared and was silent for several seconds.

"Wow. You look…wow!"

I smiled. "Glad you like it."

"Like it? I love it…I mean…WOW. You look fantastic, but…are we going someplace special?" He glanced down at his dark washed jeans, white shirt and leather jacket. "Do I need to go home and put on a suit?"

"You look fine." I put the dogs away, transferred my keys and a wallet into a small handbag and then got a lightweight jacket from the hall closet.

Red helped me on with my jacket and then turned me to face him. "Seriously, it'll just take a minute for me to change my shirt and get a tie."

"You look great." I smiled.

His expression showed he didn't believe me, so I reached up and kissed him.

We went to one of my favorite restaurants in Chattanooga which was known for its prime rib, although I was partial to the braised beef short ribs. The atmosphere was what I'd call urban casual with jazz music, soft lighting and a contemporary décor. We chatted and sipped cocktails.

Red leaned forward. "Are you going to tell me what's up?"

"What do you mean?"

He stared at my dress and I was thankful the lighting was soft and hoped it hid the color I knew was going up my neck. "You're acting like it's a crime to wear a nice dress," I teased.

He gave me a stare that caused more heat. "The way you look tonight just might be a crime." After a few moments he said, "Seriously, what's up?"

I sipped my cocktail. "I just wanted to look extra nice because I'm so thankful to have you in my life."

He leaned across and kissed me. "I'm very grateful for you too, but…"

"I appreciate you getting security for Mrs. Huntington, even though I didn't have proof. I'm grateful that you believed me, and I just wanted to look extra special, that's all."

He took my hand. "Lilly, I think you're beautiful and I'm thankful to have you in my life. However, I assigned the guard to watch Mrs. Huntington because it's my duty. If there's the slightest chance that she could be in danger, it's my job to do what I can to protect her." He gave me a hard stare. "You visited with her two days ago. You spoke on the phone to her yesterday." He paused while our waiter brought our salads. When he was gone, Red continued. "Something happened either when you saw her or when you spoke to her that made you concerned for her safety." He took a deep breath. "You may not be able to put your finger on what that thing is right now, but you have good instincts. I'd be a fool if I didn't listen."

"So, you didn't assign the security guard just because you're fond of me?" I smiled.

He grinned. "I'm more than fond of you, but…" He shook his head. "I assigned the security guard because there's a killer on the loose and I don't think I could live with myself if I did nothing and something happened to Mrs. Huntington." He got the faraway look in his eyes that came whenever he thought back on his military past.

I leaned across and kissed him. "Great. Is now a good time to ask for a favor?"

He came back to the present, shook his head and tried to stop his lips from twitching. "Go for it."

I quickly told Red what we knew about Archibald Lowry's will and did my best to explain a pour-over trust. He frowned a couple of times but seemed to get the gist of the concept. Now came the tricky part. "So, I was thinking it would be great if a CPA looked at Archibald Lowry's bank account and the trust." I scrunched my eyes and was almost afraid to look at him.

"The TBI has forensic accountants who are fully capable of reviewing Archibald Lowry's bank accounts, and I don't even know what would be involved in getting permission to review the trust." He rubbed the back of his neck. "Even if I wanted to have…" he used air quotes "an independent CPA." He took a deep breath. "It's not that easy. We would have to have probable cause that there was something fishy with his finances. Then, we would have to get a court order to look into his bank accounts and the trust, unless the estate voluntarily gave consent, which is unlikely."

"Phooey."

"Doesn't look like I'm going to be able to grant that favor." He shook his head. and started to eat. "Although, I'm still glad you bought that dress."

I laughed. "Me too."

We ate and chatted about things completely unrelated to murder until we finished our dinners. I ordered the chocolate molten lava cake with white chocolate raspberry ice cream while Red sipped coffee.

"Have you found out anything new?" I asked.

Red didn't ask what the question was in reference to. Instead, he took a sip of coffee and said, "Actually, Joe helped me realize that I've been looking for a connection between Archibald Lowry, Paul Carpenter and the rest of that lot. He suggested I take Lowry out of the equation."

I swirled the warm chocolate desert and ice cream together and took a bite. When I opened my eyes, I realized Red was laughing at me. "What?"

"Do you need a moment alone with that?" He pointed down at my dessert.

I took a spoonful of the chocolate ambrosia and fed it to him.

He moaned. "That's good stuff." He got the waiter's attention, pointed to the dessert and indicated that he wanted one. The waiter must have understood his makeshift sign language because he nodded and headed toward the back.

"So, you took Archibald Lowry out of the equation. How did that help?"

He picked up a spoon and reached across and took another bite. "Bradington went to jail for the bank robbery. There were two other people involved who were never caught and Bradington never gave them up. I looked up the officer who worked the case and gave him a call."

The waiter returned with another chocolate dessert, and Red took a minute to eat. After a few spoonfuls he continued. "Bradington wasn't the brightest dog in the pack. He was known more for his brawn rather than his brains." He took another bite. "However, there were two other men that Bradington used to spend a lot of time with. Clarence Darling, a cat burglar, and Oscar Goldstein, a jeweler and suspected fence."

I stared. "Darling and Goldstein? Any relation?"

He nodded. "Fiona Darling is a niece and Eli is Oscar Goldstein's son."

I paused with the spoon midway to my mouth. "What does that mean?"

"It might not mean anything. It might just mean that Archibald Lowry knew a lot of criminals." He shrugged. "Maybe Lowry felt sorry for them and wanted to help the offspring of a few men who made some bad choices. There's nothing that directly connects Eli Goldstein or Fiona Darling to the robbery or murder." He shook his head. "Heck, there's nothing that connected Clarence Darling or Oscar Goldstein to the robberies, or they would have served time."

"Where are they now? Clarence and Oscar?"

"Dead."

I thought about this for several moments. "Did the policeman you talked to think the three of them committed the robbery?"

"He believed the three of them were in it together, but...he didn't think they actually planned it."

"So, there was someone else?"

He nodded. "The officer I spoke with never believed he got the brains behind the operation."

Something flashed across my mind but was gone in an instant. I tried to catch it, but it was gone too quickly. Who had the *brains* to not only execute a bank heist, but the ability to keep the loot hidden for a long time?

Chapter 19

We enjoyed the rest of our evening. On the drive home, Red took my hand. "Did you really suggest Joe investigate Eli?" Red asked.

I avoided direct eye contact. "He's a suspect in a murder investigation."

He grinned. "He also happens to be dating your daughter."

"Two completely unrelated incidents."

"Careful, your nose might start growing." He smiled. After a few moments, he hesitantly added, "So, you wouldn't be upset if someone you know in law enforcement had…already done a full background check on him?"

I twisted in my seat to get a better look at his face. "Are you trying to tell me that you ran a background check on Eli Goldstein because he was dating my daughter?"

"Maybe." He gave a couple of quick glances in my direction. "I'm not admitting anything without my legal counsel present, especially if it's going to make you angry."

I tried to scowl but I couldn't maintain it. Instead, I unbuckled my seat belt, leaned over and kissed him on the cheek. "I'm going to accept that your heart was in the right place." I refastened the seat belt and leaned back. "Although, I don't think we should tell Stephanie that."

He grinned. "Fine with me."

When I got home, Stephanie was already asleep. I let Rex and Aggie out for a quick potty break before going to bed where I tossed and turned for a long time. Something was bothering me, but I couldn't put my finger on what, exactly it was. I tried to relax and let my mind drift. However, nothing came to me. Eventually, I fell asleep and dreamed of a poodle running through a field of chocolate.

Thursday morning started much the same as the previous morning. When I woke up, Stephanie and Lucky were outside on the back deck. Aggie and Rex hurried to take care of their business.

"You were home early," I said.

"Eli said he had work to do, so..." She shrugged. Then she turned her head and glanced at me. "While you, on the other hand, were out rather late."

I couldn't avoid smiling.

She leaned over and hugged me. "You and Red are so cute together. I'm really happy for you."

After a few moments, I shared what I'd learned with her.

"I'm sorry Mom, but I think Red's right. You can't look at the books... not legally anyway."

I smiled. "Well, there are other ways."

"Mother, as an attorney, I can't know anything about illegal—"

I waved away her disclaimer. "I'm your mother and a law-abiding citizen. I can't believe you think I'd do anything illegal."

She narrowed her eyes and stared, but after a few moments she said, "Good, because I think it would break Red's heart to arrest his girlfriend."

"Oh, you." I gave her a playful swat.

Dixie and I planned to stop by the hospital later in the day to see Mrs. Huntington, but other than that, I was happy to get to spend a little time with Stephanie. I fixed breakfast and we sat on the deck and talked.

The doorbell rang, and I was surprised to see Joe and Turbo on the porch.

"Joe, what a nice surprise." I stared. He looked tired as though he hadn't slept much.

"Is Stephanie here? I need to talk to her."

"She's on the deck."

He and Turbo walked back. The set of his jaw told me this was likely to be an unpleasant conversation so I decided now would be a good time to do housework. Fortunately, or unfortunately, I chose to start with laundry.

The washer and dryer were in the kitchen. By the time I finished loading the washer, I could hear raised voices from the deck.

"You were following me? I can't believe you followed me."

Joe's voice wasn't as loud, but I could easily make out what was said. "I wasn't following you. I was following Eli."

"Same difference."

"No, it's not, but the bottom line is while I was following him, I happened to see him making out with another woman, a redheaded—"

"I don't want to hear this. You have no right to spy on me or Eli."

I could tell by the edge in Stephanie's voice that she was beyond upset, although I wasn't sure if she was angry at Joe or Eli or both. I'm not sure it really mattered. I quickly got the washer started and decided now would be an excellent time to run the vacuum in my bedroom since that room was the farthest away from the back deck.

The sound of the vacuum cleaner was able to drown out their voices, and the vacuum's long cord enabled me to move from my bedroom to the guest room without stopping. After a few moments, I heard a door slam and then a car speed away. I glanced out the front window and Joe's car was gone. I vacuumed the two guest bedrooms and was about to wash windows when Stephanie came inside.

"Did you hear that?"

I thought about lying but didn't think I could pull it off. "I heard some of it."

Her face was red, and she was livid. "I can't believe he followed us. He actually followed us."

"Did he mention why?"

She paced across the floor. "Oh, he said he was tailing Eli, but I don't believe him."

"Well, honey, he is a policeman and he was probably just helping out with the investigation."

She paused. "You knew about this?"

I was taken aback by the question, but decided honesty was the best policy. "I didn't know he was going to follow Eli, but...I might have suggested he help Red with the investigation."

She stared at me openmouthed.

"Actually, I might have suggested he specifically investigate Eli."

"I can't believe you did that." She stared at me for several moments and then marched to the guest room and closed the door.

I thought about knocking on her door but didn't have the courage or the nerve. Instead, I decided to give her a little space. One thing I've learned as a parent is that sometimes time and distance can heal much better than words. Stephanie was upset, maybe rightly so. However, when she calmed down, I prayed she would realize that both Joe and I had good intentions. I could explain and apologize later.

I ran some errands which involved picking up dog food, a stop at the dry cleaners, getting my oil changed and scheduling appointments for a manicure and pedicure for the next day. Optimistically, I scheduled appointments for both me and Stephanie. Even if she was still angry with me, she probably wouldn't pass up a free mani/pedi. Dixie and I planned to stop by the hospital to check on Mrs. Huntington before dog class. However, when I got a call from Red saying she was asking for me, we changed our plans. I sent Dixie a message and she said she'd be by the house to pick me up in twenty minutes. That gave me enough time to drive home. I took the food and dry cleaning inside.

Stephanie was sitting on the deck with the three dogs.

"Red called and said that Mrs. Huntington regained consciousness enough to ask for me. Dixie and I are going to the hospital."

She looked concerned. "Is there anything you need me to do?"

I scowled as I tried to come up with the best plan. I checked my watch. "I don't know how long I'll be at the hospital. I guess I should take Aggie and Rex with me, so we don't have to drive back here before dog class. Although I'm not sure if Dixie is in the RV or her car." I pulled out my cell phone to send Dixie another text.

"Why don't I bring the dogs to the dog club?"

"That would be wonderful."

The doorbell rang.

"That must be Dixie."

I waffled for a few seconds until Stephanie said, "Go. I'll be glad to bring the dogs tonight. I don't have any other plans."

I didn't stop to think if there was another meaning behind those words. Instead, I decided to take her at face value and hurried to the door.

Dixie was driving her Lexus, so I felt much better about the decision to leave the poodles behind. I didn't want to leave them in the car, although Dixie's luxury vehicle had remote start and we could leave them with air conditioning, radio and treats, there was a huge difference between leaving them in a car versus leaving them inside of a luxury RV which has been custom designed as a poodle transportation haven.

By the time we arrived at the hospital, Mrs. Huntington wasn't in a state that I would call conscious. Instead, she waffled in between a state of semi-consciousness and deep unconsciousness.

We sat by her bedside and waited for…I don't know what to happen. After about thirty minutes, she began to toss and turn and mumbled, "Echosby."

I hopped up and hurried to her side. Clasping her hand, I said, "Yes? This is Mrs. Echosby. I'm here."

She tossed and mumbled so low I had to lean down to hear.

I bent my ear close to her mouth. Eventually, I heard. "Tea…bad… trust…Echosby."

"I'm sorry, but I don't understand."

She became more agitated.

A beep came from one of the machines connected to her and within seconds a nurse flew into the room.

I stepped away from the bed.

The nurse looked at the pulse monitor and blood pressure and pushed another button. Five more people rushed into the room. One of them was wearing a white coat, which I assumed indicated she was the doctor. The group pushed us aside and barked orders. Something was injected into the I.V.

Dixie and I stood near the wall and held hands as we watched the frantic activity around the bedside.

Within seconds the machine, which had sounded like a frantic alarm earlier, returned to a soft beep and the stress level in the room went from DEFCON one down to DEFCON five. Everyone breathed a sigh of relief and with the oxygen returning to the room I was able to breathe again.

The doctor turned to Dixie and me. "What happened?"

Dixie shrugged and I shook my head.

"I have no idea." I replayed the scene over but still couldn't figure out what had caused the huge commotion. When I thought of the fact that Mrs. Huntington could have died, I felt as if my knees would buckle from the stress. "Can I sit down?"

The doctor helped me to a seat and I flopped down. She was a petite African American woman with smooth dark skin and a small afro. She looked at me and then reached out and took my wrist and checked my pulse. She must have been satisfied because after a few moments she said, "You're going to be okay, just take deep breaths."

I followed orders and felt less shaky. "I'm sorry, doctor. Did I do something wrong?"

She shook her head. "No. She's been through a great deal of trauma. We were hoping to question her about her medical history, so we delayed putting her in a coma. Plus, the police wanted to question her. However, I no longer have that luxury. I have put her into a coma to help her brain heal so the swelling can go down, but there are no guarantees."

We asked a few more questions, but the doctor wasn't able to give us many answers. The only thing we knew for sure was that Mrs. Huntington would be in a coma for at least a week or more so it was unlikely that she would be asking for me or anyone else for quite some time.

When we left the hospital, neither one of us was feeling up to dog training. In fact, Dixie called Beau and told him not to bother bringing Chyna or Leia down the mountain for class. We stopped by the Mellow

Mushroom and ordered two pizzas and then picked up some beverages and headed to the dog club.

Everyone was already there by the time we arrived. Dixie explained that she wasn't up to teaching tonight and asked if anyone would mind if we skipped class. She promised to add an additional class or refund one week of the class fee. Of course, no one was interested in the refund.

Stephanie touched my shoulder. "Are you okay? You look pale."

I nodded. Something about the compassion in her eyes triggered a nerve and I started to weep.

Stephanie hugged me while I cried for poor Mrs. Huntington who was lying in a coma with no one to speak for her.

Eventually I took a deep breath and pushed away. "I'm sorry. I don't know what came over me."

"It's okay. I'm sorry I was such a brat earlier."

"You weren't a br—"

"Oh yes I was. I was embarrassed and angry, and I took it out on you and Joe and neither one of you deserved it."

"I shouldn't have interfered. It's just that I'm your mother and you were dating a man who was connected to a double homicide." I stared at her. "I was worried for you. I wouldn't have done it for any other reason."

She smiled. "I know."

I took a deep breath. If confession was good for the soul, then I might as well make a clean breast of everything. "However, I am dating a TBI Officer and…well, Red had already run a background check on Eli. In fact, regardless of what happens between you and Eli or Joe…I'm pretty sure he's going to run background checks on everyone you and David become involved with."

Stephanie shook her head. "It's invasive and probably unethical and possibly illegal without probable cause." She smiled. "However, I know he's only doing it from a place of love and concern."

We hugged, put the dogs outside and then sat down at the picnic table with the pizza, beer and peach wine coolers that Dixie picked up at the liquor store.

B.J. bit into a slice of pizza. "So now will you tell us what happened?"

Dixie and I took turns filling in the details.

"Good lord, I'll have to make sure to add her to the prayer list at church," Monica Jill said.

I updated the group on the information I had from Red. I tried not to keep glancing at Stephanie while I shared what I'd learned about Eli Goldstein's father, Ivan Bradington and Clarence Darling.

Dr. Morgan was also giving Stephanie a strange look. Eventually, he cleared his throat and said, "I wasn't sure if I should say anything or not, but in light of what we've learned already, I feel like I should."

Stephanie frowned. "If you know something that will help, please... go ahead."

Dr. Morgan nodded. "I'm not sure if it will help solve the murder, but Mai," he blushed. "Mr. Lowry's gamekeeper mentioned that she had seen Eli Goldstein with Fiona Darling in a very...compromising position."

Stephanie colored but reached out and patted Dr. Morgan's hand. "It's okay." She took a deep breath. "I had a lot of time alone today to think about the situation and the bottom line is, I don't really like Eli Goldstein."

I breathed a sigh of relief.

Dixie smiled. "Thank God."

Stephanie laughed. "That's a strong reaction."

"I'm sorry, dear." Dixie reached across and patted Stephanie's hand. "I didn't even get a chance to tell your mom, but earlier today I went by Signal Mountain Loan and Trust. I have a friend who works there and I asked her about Archibald Lowry's Trust. She wasn't at liberty to give me specific information, but...she did tell me that there might not be as much money in the trust as there was at one time."

"Sounds like somebody had a hand in the cookie jar," B.J. said.

Dixie nodded. "That's the exact impression I got too. In fact, she indicated," she leaned forward and whispered, "off the record of course, that I might not be able to buy a dog leash with what was left." Monica Jill sat with her mouth open.

"Close your mouth, you'll catch flies," B.J. joked with her friend.

Monica Jill put both hands on her face. "You have got to be kidding. Who could have done that?"

Stephanie glanced down. "I think I have a pretty good idea."

We all stared at her.

She took a deep breath. "I didn't want to believe it, but all of the evidence was right there in front of us. Eli Goldstein was the trustee. He had access to the trust. He's the only one who could have taken the money out."

I got a flashback and this time rather than flitting away, it stayed. "That's what bothered me when I talked to Mrs. Huntington." I stared across at Dixie. "Remember when I told you she said Eli Goldstein had told her she was getting five thousand dollars in the will."

Dixie nodded.

"Well, the will Stephanie showed us indicated he had left her ten thousand dollars."

Dixie smacked the table with her hand. "That's right. I remember now."

"That low-down dirty...thief," B.J. said.

"I'll bet he told all of the beneficiaries they were getting less than what Archibald Lowry intended and then he pocketed the money."

Dixie stared at me. "I don't think Fergus Kilpatrick would take too kindly to being swindled out of money he felt entitled to."

My brain refused to even imagine how Fergus would react.

Stephanie shook her head. "I knew there was something about Eli Goldstein that just wasn't right. He's handsome, but..."

I stared at my daughter. "You're not terribly disappointed, are you?"

"Of course not. If I'm honest with myself, I think I was just flattered by the attention. He was a boost to my ego and...maybe a small part of me wanted to make Joe jealous."

"Thank goodness." I took a deep breath.

Stephanie laughed. "He's handsome, but not very bright. I mean, he kept trying to convince me that all those red hairs on his clothes were from Lucky." She smirked. "Lucky didn't even like him and certainly wouldn't have been that close to him."

"I'm so glad you picked up on that. I meant to mention it, but you were so upset and then I got the call about Mrs. Huntington at the hospital and it completely slipped my mind."

She sighed. "Yeah, I put two and two together when Joe mentioned he saw Eli making out with a redhead." She shrugged. "I had to admit, that Eli wasn't faithful." She sighed. "Although he was certainly very handsome."

"Hmmm he sure is handsome, but that's not the kind of man you marry. That's the kind of man you fool around with." B.J. laughed. "Nah, you want someone you can count on for the long haul. Someone like that police officer of yours. Now, that's a real man." She gave Stephanie a playful shove that made her smile. "Plus, he's mighty good to look at too."

B.J. and Monica Jill joked with Stephanie about her abundance of nice-looking men which put color in her cheeks and a twinkle in her eyes. For the first time since she arrived, she looked happy.

When the joking subsided, we got serious.

"Okay, so we know Eli Goldstein can't be trusted, but that doesn't make him a murderer," Dixie said.

It doesn't, but between the red hairs, the poison, the bank robbery and the attempts to nab Rex, it's all starting to make sense. The pieces of this puzzle were finally starting to fall into place. I had a plan that just might tie up the final loose ends.

Chapter 20

It didn't take Red as long as I thought it would to agree to my plan, probably because there wasn't a whole lot to it and virtually nothing he could do to stop it. Once he was on board, he quickly set about trying to make sure the auction was surrounded by police and as safe as Fort Knox.

I spent Friday morning running errands in preparation for the auction and got so busy I almost missed my spa appointment. It wasn't until Aggie scratched my leg in her efforts to extract a treat that I remembered. Stephanie was ecstatic when I told her that I made an appointment for her too.

We hurried to the salon and indulged in a few hours of pampering and indulgence. When our feet were soft as a baby's bottom and my nails were dipped and painted a pale pink, I was ready to tackle just about anything.

We went home to shower and prepare for the big event. I thought Stephanie planned to wear the sexy red dress she bought, until she came out of the guest room wearing the beautiful navy-blue dress. She looked stunning.

I put on the dress I bought for the occasion and waited. Dixie and Beau arrived on time in the RV and Stephanie and I, along with Aggie, Rex and Lucky all climbed inside.

Dixie looked lovely and elegant. Only a close friend would notice the strained look in her eyes and the habit she had of twisting her wedding ring when she was nervous.

"Do you really think this will work?" She asked.

I shrugged. "I don't know, but it's worth a shot."

She nodded. "You're right."

Beau eased the RV into the staff lot beside the museum and we unloaded our pack.

The two standards and Lucky were so well-behaved that there wasn't much to worry about where they were concerned. Dixie had groomed the big dogs and placed red bows in their ears. They looked regal and smelled lovely.

One of my earlier errands involved dropping Rex and Aggie at the big box pet store for a bath and trim. Aggie had removed her ribbons in between leaving the pet store and our arrival home, but I had a fancy harness dress and a rhinestone leash, so she looked cute, despite her best efforts. Rex was fluffed to perfection. He had a bandana around his neck when I picked him up, but I had other plans for this little silver boy. I replaced the bandana with the jewel studded collar that Archibald Lowry gave him. I added a new electronic tracking square, which I bought with a matching rhinestone leash. Lucky's coat was beautiful and when it was brushed out thoroughly, it glistened. Aggie had a fancy black rhinestone collar that shone like diamonds.

Inside, the museum was elegantly decorated, just as it had been one week ago today. However, in addition to the decorations, catering and string quartet, there was another section of the museum which was hosting the items up for auction. I spotted Linda Kay almost immediately. She was wearing a long black dress with a sheer overlay that was set off with rhinestones around the neck and the cuffs. She sat on her scooter near a table laden with champagne glasses. She and her husband both loved dogs, so getting her to agree to allow a few well-trained dogs in the museum hadn't been hard. In fact, she and her husband brought their dog, Dingo, who was black and brown with a few white patches on his body and around his muzzle. He looked like a mix of beagle, hound and a little terrier thrown in for good measure. Dingo lay on his back, four paws in the air while Linda Kay scratched his exposed belly and talked to Jacob who was looking dapper, compression boot and all.

Monica Jill arrived wearing a stunning light blue dress with a diagonal ruffle that zig zagged the left side of the dress and made her look even slimmer and taller than she already was. The three-inch heels didn't hurt either. Next to Monica Jill was Addison, in a simple yellow dress and ballet flats.

When she got a glimpse of our pack, she hurried to pet the dogs. "They look so cute and soft." She leaned down and Aggie proceeded to lick every surface of her face.

"Addy, I'm so glad you were able to come and help us with the dogs." Dixie reached down and gave the girl a hug.

"I love dogs and I was so excited with Miss Monica Jill asked me." She looked over at Monica Jill. "I just wish you had brought Jac." She pouted.

Monica Jill shook her head. "No. We are only bringing well-behaved dogs tonight." She chuckled. "I love that dog, but...no way would I trust him in a place like this." She glanced at Dixie. "Not yet, anyway."

Dixie gave her a smile and then nudged me. "What a difference a week makes."

I followed her glance and saw a confident Dr. Morgan arrive along with his German shepherd, Max. He was wearing a black suit and looked nice. However, the twinkle in his eyes was more than likely caused by the fact that on his arm was Mai Nguyen.

I spied Red and Joe standing in a corner. He must have felt my glance because he looked across at me. He whispered something to Joe and then sauntered over. When he arrived, he greeted everyone and then leaned down and gave me a quick kiss and whispered, "You look amazing."

I smiled. "Thank you." I had been confident of my plan yesterday. Now, I was filled with doubt. "Do you think this will work?"

He shrugged. "I hope so."

Joe and Turbo stood near the door. Joe was dressed in jeans and a jacket and was clearly there for security rather than as a guest. Turbo was wearing his vest which indicated he was working.

After a few moments, Red beckoned for Joe to join us.

Reluctantly, he and Turbo joined our small group. "Hello." He greeted each of us, but his eyes lingered the longest on Stephanie. "You look... beautiful."

"Thank you."

After a few seconds of uncomfortable silence, she turned to Red. "I know Joe's working, but can I have a word with him?"

Red nodded his consent.

Joe looked worried.

"Come with me." Stephanie and Lucky waltzed over to an empty corner while Joe and Turbo followed.

We shamelessly watched the two and after a few moments were all pleased to see a smile break out on Joe's face followed by the two embracing and then sharing a passionate kiss. "Aww," the women all said at the same time.

"Great. Now, my security is going to be distracted," Red joked.

I gave him a playful elbow and he laughed.

At that moment, Mary and Fergus Kilpatrick approached our group. Fergus stared at Rex. "Well, hello there." He reached out a hand to pet Rex and I forced myself to resist the impulse to pull him away.

Rex submitted to the petting, which I'm sure he felt was his due.

"Have you come to hand him over?" He reached for Rex and this time I did pull away.

Fergus gave a fake laugh. "My wife just loves that dog and it would break her heart to have to give him up, but I'm sure we can resolve this like civilized people and come to terms that will be agreeable to everyone, without involving the law."

Mary Kilpatrick had been drinking champagne during the entire conversation and staring at Red with a come hither look in her eyes. At her husband's words, she stopped staring long enough to glance in Rex's direction. "Oh yes, I just love her. She's so cute."

Addison giggled. "Rex is a boy."

Dixie mumbled. "*Wisdom oft comes from the mouth of babes.*"

I frowned. "I'm not familiar with that quote. That's not Shakespeare, is it?"

She shook her head. "*Game of Thrones.*"

I nodded. "Fitting."

Eli Goldstein, dressed fashionably in a black suit with his hair pulled back into a man bun, joined our group. "Ah…if it isn't my favorite people."

The dogs all growled and we each increased the hold we had on our animals.

He chuckled. "What is it about these dogs? They just don't seem to like me." He shook his head. "Is it my cologne?"

He reached out to pet Rex, but a rumble from the two standard poodles and Aggie made him withdraw his hand.

Fergus glanced at Eli. "I've just been explaining to Mrs. Echosby how attached Mary is to the little…guy. Maybe you can—"

Stephanie returned to the group, hand in hand with Joe and followed by Lucky and Turbo. "Mr. Kilpatrick, I've made it clear through your attorney," she nodded toward Eli, "that my mom has no intention of giving up her dog. If you continue to harass her, then I'll be forced to file a restraining order against you."

Fergus Kilpatrick's eyes flashed and his jaw hardened. He lifted a finger as though to point it in Stephanie's direction and in less than a split second, Joe and Turbo were in front of Stephanie.

"I sure hope you weren't about to point that finger toward the lady." Joe gave the older man a cold hard stare. His body was tense and the edge in his voice made the hair on my arms stand up. He had flipped the switch and was one hundred percent cop.

Even Turbo sensed the change in his partner. His body shook from the pent-up nervous energy and it was clear that one word from Joe would send him flying at Fergus Kilpatrick's throat.

After what felt like forever, but was only seconds, Fergus Kilpatrick lowered his hand.

Eli gave a nervous laugh. "I think my clients need a moment to cool down." He guided Fergus and Mary away by the arm. Before he left, he turned to Stephanie and looked her up and down like a piece of meat. Then he grinned. "You look nice," he said, then walked away.

After he left, I heard Dixie let out a sigh and only then did I release the breath I was holding.

Joe turned to Stephanie. "Are you okay?"

"I'm fine." She shivered. "I just can't believe I ever thought that louse was attractive."

I hadn't even heard B.J.'s arrival until she spoke. "Isn't it funny how someone can seem so attractive one minute and the next minute all you can see is the dirt on the inside."

"What a jerk. Did you see the way he looked Stephanie up and down like a prized heifer at a 4-H fair?" Monica Jill put her hand on her hip.

"Yeah, I saw it," Joe mumbled. "I should have let Turbo take that smile off his face."

Red patted him on the back. "Alright, remember you're working."

Joe nodded. After a few moments, he turned to me. "What now?"

"It's time for the auction." Dixie glanced at her watch and then hurried off.

"It's show time." Beau took Chyna and Leia's leashes.

I handed Rex and Aggie to Addison and Mai. Dr. Morgan took Lucky and Max and they all headed out back to the RV.

Part of my plan involved the dogs, specifically Rex, being left with minimal supervision. However, now that the time had come for implementation, I was having second thoughts. Stephanie must have noticed the fear in my eyes, because she hugged me and whispered, "It'll be okay."

I took a deep breath and nodded. Addison and Mai were to be seen taking the dogs to the RV but then would return to the auction. Beau and Dr. Morgan were to take turns watching the RV and being seen in the museum. Plus, I knew Red had police dispatched around the building watching the RV while he, Joe and a half-dozen plainclothes officers kept their eyes on Eli and Fergus Kilpatrick.

Once the auction began it went well. Periodically, I glanced around to make sure I knew exactly where Eli and Fergus Kilpatrick were. After a while, I got wrapped up in the bidding and almost forgot about the poodle trap. It wasn't until I noticed Red talking to someone through a wireless Bluetooth audio device that I became concerned. One of the waiters approached Eli and grasped him by the arm and another guest escorted Fergus out back. It was all done quickly and with very little attention. I doubted that any of the guests even knew what was happening. I

Red exchanged a few words with Joe and then they both rushed out the back.

One of the stipulations I made to get Red to agree to my plan was a promise to stay inside when I saw things start to go down. I tried to keep that promise, but things were not going the way I planned. Eli and Fergus hadn't gone for the dogs.

Stephanie whispered in my ear. "What just happened?"

I looked around carefully. "It's Fiona and Mary. They're not here." That's when I broke my word and rushed outside.

Stephanie and I arrived at the RV to find Dr. Morgan and Beau on the ground, bound with dog leashes.

I hurried over to them. "Are you two okay?"

Both men nodded. There was a trickle of blood coming from Beau's forehead, but otherwise he looked fine.

"Where are Addison and Mai?" I glanced around frantically.

Dr. Morgan coughed and spit blood. "Addison's fine. She's inside." He inclined his head toward the museum.

Red had been standing nearby talking to one of the policemen. He came over and said, "They took Mai and Rex. We have the GPS tracker on the dog." He pulled up his cell phone. "We're tracking them and we're going to get them both back. Now, go back inside and let me do my job." He gave me a hard stare.

I nodded.

He gave me another look and then he, Joe and Turbo took off on foot.

Dr. Morgan was helping Beau into the RV to treat the cut on his forehead.

I stood outside for several minutes. This was my fault. This was my plan. Now, thanks to me two of my friends were injured. Rex and Mai were in danger. For several moments, I wallowed in guilt and self-doubt. Afterward, I heard the dogs barking in the RV and my mom Spidey sense kicked in. I recognized Aggie's bark in the cacophony of barking dogs.

I went to the RV and opened the door.

Like a flash of lightning, Aggie raced down the steps and took off.

"Aggie. Come back." I chased after her but in heels I knew I'd never catch her.

I removed my shoes and then hopped in the RV.

"Mom, what happened?" Stephanie asked.

"Aggie just took off and I think I know where she went." I looked at the RV's complex cockpit and for a few seconds, my courage faltered.

That's when Stephanie hiked up her dress, kicked off her shoes and slid into the driver's seat. She started the engine, took two seconds to find the right controls and then strapped her seat belt. "You better buckle up. This might be bumpy."

I grabbed my seat belt and fastened it. Then I pulled out my cell phone. My hands shook and I struggled to enter my passcode. After a couple failed attempts, I used the fingerprint access instead. Once, I was in, I quickly found the GPS tracking app for the device on Rex's collar. When I had the app up and running, I turned to Stephanie. "They're headed to the river."

Chapter 21

I talked Stephanie through the directions to the Tennessee River and she maneuvered the 30-foot vehicle with four adults and four barking dogs.

When we pulled up to the river, we saw Red, Joe and Turbo along with a crowd of police with guns pointed toward Fiona who had removed Rex's collar and was holding him up by the scruff of his neck with a crazed look in her eye. Mary Kilpatrick had her arm around Mai's neck and a gun pointed at her head.

I opened the door to the RV and hopped out. Red glanced around and, seeing me, he shook his head and yelled, "Stay back."

I froze.

Fiona extended her hand so Rex was now dangling over the river. She snarled, "Stay back or I might just lose my grip and drop him." For a brief second, my mind cleared and remembered Dixie mentioning the gun Beau kept in the glove box. I leaned back in the vehicle and slowly and quietly opened the glove box. I reached my hand in the glove box until I felt the gun.

"Drop your weapons on the ground or I'll blow her brains out," Mary Kilpatrick yelled.

Red and the other officers delayed until Mary fired a shot into the air. The blast from the gun and the crazy look in her eyes must have convinced them that she meant business.

Turbo was growling and barking and lunging toward Mary, but Joe held onto him.

"Keep that dog away or I'll kill her," Mary yelled.

Red tried to rationalize and get Mary to drop the gun and let Rex and Mai go, but both women were beyond reasonable thought.

"Shut up," Fiona yelled. "I've waited too many years to get my hands on this." She held up Rex's collar. "There's no way I'm walking away without it."

I hid the gun by my side and took several steps forward. I could tell that Red saw what I was doing, but he gave no indication of anything happening behind the women.

"Why did you kill Archibald Lowry and Paul Carpenter?" Red kept their attention focused on him.

Fiona cackled. "I didn't kill Lowry or Carpenter." She spat. "That was Eli. We've been poisoning him for months with arsenic while we tried to figure out what the old man did with the money." She shook her head. "That was the plan, poison him slowly and then when we got the rest of the money, one big dose. Clean and easy with no blood and no mess, but he couldn't wait." She snarled with disgust. "Eli had to get greedy and start siphoning the money out of the trust." She snorted. "How dumb. Of course, Archibald found out and put two and two together."

From the corner of my eye, I saw Aggie crouched down by a concrete pillar behind Fiona. She was on her stomach like a sphinx and was crawling on her belly, inching closer and closer to Fiona the way Chyna and Leia did when going through the crawl tunnel in the agility ring.

"We knew there was more money than what he had in that trust. He had the money from the bank robbery. We just needed to find out what he'd done with it. Eli went to the art museum and Lowry told him he knew he'd been draining the trust and he intended to stop him. They argued and Eli killed him. Right before he died, he saw the jewels in the collar and figured out what the old man had done." Fiona stared at the collar and then smiled at Red. "Now, we have it."

Mary laughed. "That's why we needed to get our hands on that blasted dog. Once we found out what that old man had done, putting the jewels out in plain sight on that dog, we just needed to get him and then be on our way."

I took a few more steps forward but stepped on a leaf which sounded like a bomb exploding in the quiet of the night.

Fiona turned. "What are you going to do?"

I pointed the gun at her.

Red shouted, "Lilly, no!"

Fiona laughed. "If you shoot me. I might just lose my grip on this little rat." She shook Rex and my heart skipped a beat when I heard him yelp.

Mai gave a loud yell. "NOW!" Then she bent forward and kicked her head backward, head butting Mary.

Mary screamed, and in one smooth, quick move, Mai reached up and pulled back on Mary's fingers. We heard a crunch and Mary slumped to the ground.

Fiona glanced over toward Mary and that's when Joe released Turbo who took one flying leap toward Fiona and bit down on her arm.

Fiona opened her hand. Rex let out a scream and then splashed down into the river.

Joe commanded Turbo to release his hold while he moved in and secured Fiona down onto the ground.

The other officers swarmed forward and secured Mary who was rolling on the ground, screaming in pain.

Red began removing his shirt and shoes, prepared to jump in the water.

That's when I saw a blur from the corner of my eye as Aggie took a flying leap from the pier and leapt into the water.

"Aggie, Noooo," I screamed.

Stephanie opened the RV door and yelled, "Lucky, go."

Like a golden flash, Lucky flew past me and leapt into the water as well.

My knees buckled and I collapsed. Red hesitated for a split second, unsure whether to come to me or save my dogs.

Stephanie rushed to my side and put her arms around me. "I've got Mom. Save Rex," she called to Red.

He nodded and then dove down into the black murky depths of the Tennessee River.

Chapter 22

Sirens blared. Lights flashed.

I have no idea how long I sat on the ground, but eventually I looked up and saw Red, soaking wet, walking toward me with two drenched dogs clutched to his chest. Beside him, Lucky shook several times and then trotted over to Stephanie who threw both arms around his neck.

I wrapped my arms around Red, nearly crushing the poodles. "Are you okay?"

Red nodded. "I'm fine."

I held onto him and the poodles for several seconds until an EMT rushed up and threw a blanket around his shoulders. "I'm sorry. You must be freezing."

He smiled. "Actually, I'm feeling pretty warm right now."

I laughed. "If you're well enough to joke then you must be okay."

He handed Aggie and Rex to me and I clutched them to my chest.

"I've got to go." He motioned toward the police and when I nodded, he left.

I glanced up. Dr. Morgan embraced Mai. Stephanie embraced Lucky, and I hugged my two poodles.

Later, Stephanie, Red, Joe and I sat in the RV drinking hot coffee. Red took a hot shower and changed into a pair of Beau's clothes, which were too big but had the advantage of being dry, while Dixie put his into the RV's dryer.

Joe had an arm draped around Stephanie while she rested her head on his shoulder. Lucky was sprawled across her lap and Turbo was lying next to Joe with his head on Joe's leg.

Dixie hovered over Beau who had a bandage over the cut on his head.

Mai and Dr. Morgan were snuggled together and he had a tight grip on her hand.

Rex was still shivering as he lay on my shoulder and Aggie was asleep on my lap.

Addison sat cross legged on the floor with Chyna and Leia while Monica Jill and B.J. sat at the dining room table.

"Will someone tell me what happened?" Monica Jill ordered.

Red looked around and then began to explain. "Eli and Fergus saw that we were watching them, so they got Mary and Fiona to go for the dog."

B.J. shook her head. "Ain't that just like a man, leaving the dirty work to the women."

Red smiled. "I think Eli just intended for them to get the collar away from Rex. He swears he didn't order them to take anyone hostage."

Monica Jill turned to Mai. "How did you end up getting taken as a hostage?"

Mai shrugged. "When Fiona busted into the RV, she tried to take Rex. I wasn't about to let her have him. That's when Mary came in with the gun and said, 'Let's just take her too. We might need a hostage.'"

"Where did you learn to fight like that?" Stephanie asked.

Mai smiled. "Two years in Her Majesty's Armed Forces."

Dr. Morgan gawked. "You're just full of surprises."

B.J. turned to me. "So, Lilly was right? Archibald Lowry was the brains behind the bank robbery?"

Red nodded. "Eli Goldstein is spilling his guts. According to him, Lowry was the brains behind the entire thing. Clarence Darling and Ivan Bradington were the muscle, but things went badly and Bradington shot the bank teller. The police got him, but he served his time and kept his mouth shut."

B.J. snorted. "I'll bet he kept his mouth shut."

Red smiled. "He never ratted out his partners, but that didn't help him while he was sitting in jail. Clarence Darling and Oscar Goldstein died."

"Fiona Darling was a niece and Darling told her everything. Apparently, Oscar Goldstein told Eli. When they were old enough, they both went to Lowry expecting a cut."

"Keep your friends close and your enemies closer," I said. Red stared at me. "That's what Archibald Lowry said to me that night at the museum." I turned to Dixie. "Remember, he said, 'People always ask me how I made my money'. Remember what he said?"

She thought for a moment. "He said, 'The same way every other person has become rich. I stole it.'"

I nodded.

B.J. stared. "So, Lowry took the bank money while Ivan Bradington went to jail. Bradington gets out and then comes and works for Lowry?" She shook her head. "That don't seem right."

We turned to Red. "Apparently, Lowry told him the money was tied up in investments, real estate and businesses. I don't think he told them about the jewels, or they would have figured out about the collar sooner. Bradington was pushing Lowry to divest and give him his share."

"In the meantime, Eli and Fiona had partnered to get more than the share they felt was owed to them on behalf of their uncle and father. They wanted the whole lot," Joe said.

"Fiona got a job with the bank's insurance company so she could keep an eye on things and make sure no one else got close to the money." I turned to B.J. "Remember, you said your contacts from the insurance company felt she was too close to the case."

B.J. nodded. "Well, I'll be."

"Why'd they kill Paul Carpenter?" Monica Jill asked.

"Remember at the dog show, he said 'I don't claim to be something I'm not. I don't argue with someone and once he's dead pretend that we didn't disagree.'" I think Eli was afraid that Carpenter had seen and heard too much."

Red nodded. "He heard Eli talking to Fergus and realized they weren't Lowry's relatives, nor were they running a legitimate foundation."

"Who were they?" I asked.

"Fergus and Mary were grifters," Red said.

"What's a grifter?" Dixie asked.

"A con artist," Stephanie, Joe and Red all said together and then laughed.

Dixie glanced at me. "That explains the mixed-up accents."

Red stretched. "Grifters are often great actors."

"Eli defended him when he was just starting out. Later, he looked him up and promised him a cut of the money. Eli set up the phony foundation and the story about Mary and Fergus as distant relatives. He knew Lowry was goofy over all things Scottish." He shrugged. "I guess he figured worst case scenario, if he killed Lowry and all of his wealth went to the foundation, then he would still be able to get his hands on the money."

I shivered. "So, they killed the chauffeur, Carpenter, because he overheard them talking and figured out what they were up to."

Joe nodded. "Plus, Carpenter was an extortionist. Once a blackmailer, always a blackmailer."

Dixie turned to Red. "Mrs. Huntington?"

"She saw Mary and Fergus poisoning Lowry's tea." He shrugged. "Or they thought she saw them."

"So, they really did push that poor woman down a flight of stairs?" Monica Jill asked.

Red nodded. "Pushed her and then planted the flask filled with alcohol so we'd think she tripped."

Addison yawned.

Monica Jill looked at her watch. "Oh my God. I didn't realize how late it was. I'd better get this girl home before her father strangles me."

Addison stretched. "Do we have to go? I want to hear more."

"Yes, we have to go. I have to try and explain all of this to your father, so get moving." Monica Jill grabbed her purse and a reluctant Addison and they left.

B.J. stood up. "I need to get out of here too. Snoball will be mad that I left her so long and will most likely have left me a package to clean up." She waved goodbye and left.

Dr. Morgan and Mai were the next to leave, taking Max and Skye with them, but not before Mai promised to stop by the police station the next day to complete her statement.

Red's phone rang and he stepped outside to take his call. After a few moments, he stuck his head in the door and asked me to step outside.

Once we were outside, he stared at me. "You promised me you'd stay in the museum."

I felt a flush of heat rise from my neck because I knew I had gone back on my word. I searched for some way to get out of the mess, but nothing came. I forced myself to look him in the eyes. "I'm sorry."

He stared at me. "That's it?"

I nodded. "I shouldn't have lied, but…I heard Aggie barking and when we opened the door she flew out and that's when I realized that almost everyone I cared about was out there and in danger." I looked up at him.

He leaned close. "Everyone?"

I smiled. "*Almost* everyone. Rex, Aggie…" I gazed into his eyes. "And you."

He pulled me close and kissed me. When he released me, he stared into my eyes. "Lilly Ann Echosby, I think I'm falling in love with you."

I smiled. "When you jumped into the river to save Rex and Aggie, I knew that I loved you."

He wrapped me in his arms and kissed me hard. When we finally came up for air, we stood there in the night air and held onto each other.

He nuzzled my neck. "You know, that little Aggie is something else. I couldn't believe it when she leapt into the water. That's one amazing little dog. She's fearless."

I smiled. "She takes after her namesake."

He shook his head. "No, I think she takes after her owner."

I looked up at him and traced the scar that ran along the right side of his face. "I'm not fearless. I was very afraid for you."

He took my hand and kissed me again. When we separated, we held each other and gazed at the sunrise over the Tennessee River. I thought of my family and friends and my heart was filled with love. I said a silent prayer of thanks for love and new beginnings in my *happy place.*